Books by Betty K. Erwin

AGGIE, MAGGIE, AND TISH
SUMMER SLEIGH RIDE
WHERE'S AGGIE?
BEHIND THE MAGIC LINE
GO TO THE ROOM OF THE EYES

Go to the

Room of the Eyes

Go to
the Room of
the Eyes

»»»» by Betty K. Erwin «««««

Illustrated by Irene Burns

Little, Brown and Company
BOSTON · TORONTO

3/2/70
4.95

Published simultaneously in Canada
by Little, Brown & Company (Canada) Limited

PRINTED IN THE UNITED STATES OF AMERICA

Go to the

Room of the Eyes

>>>>>>> I <<<<<<<

THIS IS the story of what happened to us when we moved to the city. It is a sad, but (we think) exciting story. We thought of calling it "We Move to the City and Everyone Hates Us," but that seemed, although descriptive, too depressing, especially to us. The setting for this story is Seattle, a rapidly growing city in the State of Washington, said by many to be the most beautiful city in the world. The characters are the members of our family, numbering eight, surname Evans. There are Mom and Dad, of course, and six children: from oldest to youngest, Susan, Katie and Dave (twins), May, Jody, and Dinky. We are nothing much to look at and until we moved to the city we thought we were exactly like everybody else.

When Dad said we were going to move we all said we wouldn't do it. May said wild horses wouldn't drag her from her dear little house and Dave said he would go around among his friends until he found someone who would take him in. Katie said they had studied city problems in school and cities were all rotten at the core, with smog and no water, and she wouldn't go and live in a slum with nothing to breathe but noxious vapors.

"Nonsense," Mom said, "there's plenty of air in Seattle. It's the same air we have here. And almost too much water. And miles and miles of beautiful old houses just waiting for someone to reclaim them. Why, it says right here," she picked up a copy of *House Beautiful* and rattled it, "that there's a great 'back to the city' movement. People are tired of driving all the time and living in those skimpy little houses. In the city you can walk or take the bus. We'll be close to shops and museums and theatres. . . ."

"But what about our friends?" Dave said. "I would much rather be close to them than to some old museums, for heaven's sake!"

"You'll make new friends," Dad said, in the same tone in which he says "Just take a taste and you'll like it." We would never grow to like broccoli and we would never, we knew in our hearts, make new friends. But when Dad talked that way there was no use arguing.

There are a lot of magazine articles claiming that modern children are allowed to make all the decisions, but of course they are wrong. When parents really make up their minds, children are helpless. They might let you decide what cereal you have for breakfast, providing it isn't too expensive or too sweet, but in any larger decisions you have no voice at all.

So we didn't bother to say anything. We thought of leaving the house where we had always lived and school and all our friends. We thought how mean it was of Mom and Dad to drag us away from everything we were used to. And then a funny thing happened. In the midst of thinking how awful it all was, we began to think it would be sort of exciting! Think of each having his own room, and living in a big house with an attic and old-fashioned things like window seats and bay windows and porches. We could go downtown alone and explore all those shops we never have a chance to go to.

"Think of being able to shop at the Market," Mom was saying.

"Everybody knows," May said, "that it is better for children to grow up in the country."

"Nonsense," Dad said. "The city is full of kids. Besides, this isn't country anymore. Look out there." He waved his hand toward the window, which gave us a grand view of the bulldozers knocking over the last of the trees. It was true. The woods and fields had disappeared year by year, and now our house in the country was surrounded by new developments.

"In fact," Dad said, "so many people are moving

over here, it ought to be quite empty and peaceful in the middle of town."

"And we're so crowded," Mom said. "This house is simply bulging. We can't all get into the dining ell anymore, and we must have more bedrooms."

"Then why did we have so many children?" Kate asked. "Why not just the top three?"

"Why not just Dave and me?" Jody asked.

"Or just Dinky and me," May said.

"It's too late to talk about that," Dad said. "Six children is not so many. All we need is seven bedrooms, that's all. Now everyone hush up. I'm going to read the house ads, and tomorrow we'll get in touch with a realtor. You kids can begin cleaning up around here. We'll have to sell this house, you know. Everything will have to be in apple-pie order. Dave, you can start on the lawn."

"*I* can start on the lawn!" Dave said. "*You* want to move, but I get to do the work. Talk about having to dig your own grave!"

"That's enough!" Dad said. "We've talked it all over, haven't we? We've had a family conference, haven't we, and decided things in a democratic way?"

"But . . ."

"It's all settled. Run along, run along. All settled. American way. Now give me the paper. Let me see those ads."

The next day there was a "For Sale" sign in our front yard.

2

AFTER THAT Mom and the baby went into town every day, looking at houses. Sometimes she didn't get back home until we were home from school, and then it was a job to get the shopping and the laundry done and something on the table for dinner. During dinner she would tell us about houses she'd seen.

"This one was a lovely big house but it had been half decorated, so that you went from a beautiful modern kitchen to the basement stairs that were like the Black Hole of Calcutta. And they'd made a modern stairway in the front hall, very odd. The worst thing was that they'd sold lots (it used to be an estate) and this high old house was surrounded by little low houses, like a hen with chicks."

Or "The next one had fireplaces in the bedrooms, so divine, but none of them worked. Imagine, all those pretty mantels and you couldn't build a fire anywhere."

Or "The next one was on the Sound. It was four stories high, with the bottom story on the beach and the top at the level of the road. You bring the groceries in at the top level, which is all right because that's the kitchen. Then you go down and down, two rooms to a floor, to the living room on the beach. I loved it, but it wasn't big enough."

We couldn't help being interested. We had never realized before that people lived in such different ways. Where we lived everyone lived just like everyone else, with a ranch house, two cars, and a boat. People in the city seemed to do just what they pleased.

"Now this house," Mom would say, "had a gymnasium, but only four bedrooms."

"This one had an observatory and a greenhouse, but it would need a new roof and the whole front had settled."

Finally there came a Friday when she said, "Now tomorrow I'm going to see a big old house on Capitol Hill. It's empty, so there won't be anything you kids can break. How would it be if we all went?"

"What's it like?" Dad asked. "How big and how old?"

"I'm not going to tell you a thing about it," Mom said. "In the first place I don't know much; the realtor was very vague. He just said it was very big and very cheap."

"Sounds good," Dad said.

"Could we each have our own room?" Susan asked.

"With some left over," Mom said. "Now I'm going to take a bath and go to bed. That last house I looked at today, the dirt, you can't imagine."

"Some left over?" Dave said. "You mean there are more than seven bedrooms?"

"Certainly," Mom said. "Put Dinky to bed, will you, Susan?"

"In the basement, I suppose. I'll probably have to sleep in the basement," Dave said gloomily.

"I never count basements," Mom said. She could be heard running bath water. "Or attics," she said.

"What did she say?" Dave asked.

"She said she wasn't counting basements or attics," Dad said. "Let's hope it has a basement and an attic. Kind of fun, eh, kids? What I want, you know, is a library. Do you think that's too much to ask? I work hard, I'm growing old. I just would like . . ."

" 'A little bit of butter to my bread,' " Susan said. "I think you should have a library, Dad, if you want one that badly." As for Susan, she had a private dream. For years, sharing a room with Kate and sometimes May, she had thought about a room of her own. Nothing startling, really. A canopy bed, flowered wallpaper, ruffled curtains, and a fireplace.

"Come on, babe," Susan said to Dinky, "let's go to bed. You can dream of a nice pink room of your own."

"I don't want a room alone," Dinky said. She was

three, and far too old to be called a baby. Her eyes filled with tears. "I want to sleep in a room with everyone else."

"You'll love it," Susan said. "You can have those junior twin beds. Two beds, just think!"

"If I wet one," Dinky said, "can I move into the other?"

"I don't know," Susan said, "but you'll have room for all your dolls and animals and things."

"If I could just have a kangaroo," Dinky said, "a nice little kangaroo to sleep with me, maybe it wouldn't be so bad."

"Go to bed," Dad said. "Just go to your lair and go to sleep."

"I just love kangaroos," Dinky said.

>>>>>> **3** <<<<<<

THE NEXT morning Jody took down the "For Sale" sign and hid it and then he ran away himself, because he said he didn't want to move ever, ever, ever. By the time Dad had found the sign and pounded it back in and the rest of us had found Jody, we were all pretty tired and consequently quiet. We sat very still, jammed in our accustomed places in the station wagon. But as we flew along the winding roads, staring blankly at the misty spring greens and the soft gray skies, we got more and more excited and the air grew thick with unspoken wishes.

"Roll down the window," Dad said. "It's getting stuffy in here."

"It's the hopes and fears," Mom said. "Now I would like a pantry."

"I would like a playroom," Jody said, "where I never had to put away my toys."

"I would like a gym," Dave said.

"A gym!" Dad said. "That's stretching it, isn't it?"

"I don't see," Dave said, "why a house big enough to have seven bedrooms not in the basement shouldn't have a basement big enough for a gym."

"By George, that's so!" Dad said. "With a dart board and pool table and weights and tumbling mats."

Then we were on the floating bridge. The bridge sat low on the water, like a duck, and the gray waves splashed it. In the sky the clouds and mountains mixed so you couldn't tell one from the other. The air came in the window, cool and wet. We looked ahead to where the city climbed its hills. Then we were off the bridge and in the tunnel.

"Hold your breath," Dad said. This was an old game.

We were through the tunnel and breathing again. We looked around.

"I knew it," May said disgustedly. "Slums!"

"These are not slums," Dad said. "You kids have never seen a slum. This is a commercial district."

"I know where we are," Dave said. "Pretty soon we'll pass that place where they have the stuffed animals." We watched for it and there it was, with a polar bear standing up and an ibex running in place. Then we passed a lot of apartment houses and houses with shops in the basement and signs reading "Cabinet Maker" or "Violin Maker," and several beautiful big houses painted clever colors like olive green or charcoal brown, saying "Architect" or "Decorators." Then came streets of big old-fashioned houses, rather shabby, with yards full of rhododendrons and tricycles. We turned some corners and stopped.

"Here we are," Dad said.

The realtor came down the front steps and opened the door of our car.

"Here we are," he said in a hearty, juicy-fruit sort of voice, "here we are. It's a grand house for kids. A great house for children. Come on, leap out and let's look around."

We hopped out, the six of us and Mother and Dad. We stood and looked.

There are lots of houses like it in the middle of town, and there were more before they started tearing them down to build freeways and high-rise apartments. It wasn't a town house at all. It looked like a country house, and we realized that it had been built when Capitol Hill was almost country. You could see that someone had built it just to please himself, because it was no style at all. It wasn't Georgian Colonial or Dutch Colonial or Queen Anne. Someone had said, "I want a big comfortable house that will last forever," and here it was, built like a rock. It was covered in weathered cedar shake, dark brown, because it was a Seattle house, and there were four big pillars on the front, probably because whoever built it liked pillars. There were porches and balconies and gables and bay windows.

You could see right away what it must have been like when it was new. There would have been cable cars then, and a livery stable around the corner. The lady of the house would have worn a long dress and high shoes. There would be three maids and a gardener and a handyman. The balconies would be gay with potted plants, and the front steps new and square, not cracked and mossy as they were now.

We went up the front steps in a body, past cement urns in which dead shrubs bristled, past an overgrown holly tree and straggling rhododendrons. We went between the pillars to the front door. It was a very big door. The realtor went first and put on the lights.

It was colder in the house than outside. The air was damp and smelled of wet fireplace ashes.

"Now," the realtor said, "this is the hall, of course. It's, er, well, it's empty, of course."

"Gosh, yes," Dave said, "it's the emptiest place I've ever been."

"Now, living room on the right, dining room on the left, library straight ahead. Kitchen behind the dining room."

Dad headed straight for the library, went in and closed the door. Mom wandered off toward the kitchen. The younger children shot up the stairs and disappeared. Susan stood shivering in the hall and looked around. The big square hall was paneled in dark wood. Dark! Even the great window on the stair landing couldn't light it. She looked at the huge living-room fireplace and at the bay window in the dining room. She looked at the dusty oak floors and thought of all the people who had lived here. She heard her mother in the kitchen, saying, "Would you believe two pantries?" She heard Jody shout, from somewhere high above, "Here's the playroom!"

So Dad had his library and Mom her pantry and Jody his playroom. Heavens, Susan thought, I'd better hurry and find my room!

So that is how we found our new house.

»»»»» **4** «««««

MOVING is so awful that we are not going to write much about it. Those months during which we cleaned our old house all day so that we could move out of it and then cleaned our new house so that we could move into it, and sorted and packed and threw away, were so full of work and strain that even Mom and Dad began to fight a little. Jody, who had been reading *Mrs. Piggle-Wiggle*, thought at first that it was the fighters-quarrelers cure, but it was for real. It is socially acceptable for adults to get mad at children because that is called discipline, but when adults get mad at each other it is embarrassing. Dad wanted to keep everything and Mom wanted to throw everything away. In the end we seemed to do both, several times over.

But there came a day, at last, when the moving van came and all our possessions were loaded in. Heavens, how shabby our furniture looked when it was moved out into the yard. We hoped our new neighbors wouldn't see it when we moved it in, but of course they did. We saw their curtains moving. Though our old house had seemed very full of furniture, it didn't go far in the new one. It was like dressing an elephant in children's clothes — great bare patches. But Mom and Dad became very gay and ran from room to room in a childish way, shoving furniture around and laughing.

By the time we moved it was late summer, but still cold and rainy. It was one of those years when there was no summer. There was no winter either. It was just November all year that year. Dad built big fires in all the fireplaces. The big chimneys drew like crazy. The air grew warm, and as the day faded outside, the house began to come alive. You could feel it stretching and sighing and saying, "Well, here we go again."

We looked forward to going to bed, each in our own room. But when the time came we couldn't sleep. Our vast unfamiliar rooms were frightening. For the first time in our lives, perhaps, we Evanses were lonely. We missed other Evanses. One by one, we got out of bed, gathered blankets or sleeping bags, and crept down the long hall to Susan's room. Dinky and Jody got into bed with Susan, one on each side of her. The rest of us slept on the floor in front of her fireplace.

Here we were, we Evans children. We learned a sad truth: when you move you have only your family. For better or for worse, that's it. We had no friends, we had to go to strange schools, tomorrow would bring a new life. We huddled together and waited for it.

And the house, perhaps fretful at being disturbed, or maybe grateful for being warmed and full of life, made little, gentle, clucking house sounds — a dripping tap somewhere, a creaking beam, a tapping bush, rain on the upstairs porch. The old roof sheltered us, the posts and beams and solid floors supported us. In the fitful firelight, on the rock-hard floor and in Susan's narrow bed, we slept.

Sleeping with Dinky and Jody was like sleeping between a hot-water bottle and a bag of tacks. The next morning Susan was glad to get them up and out and the rest of the kids out of her room too. It was a cloudy, restful morning, not raining. She lay flat on her back for a long time, looking at the cracks in the ceiling, and at the faded wallpaper and gray woodwork. She wanted to get started papering and painting right away. She could get new curtains with her babysitting money. And those shades, why, they must be the original ones, yellow, dusty, and falling to pieces. She jumped off her bed and went to the window. She yanked at the shade.

The shade came down very quickly, ripped off the

roller, and fell on the floor in a pile of dust. A scrap of paper came from somewhere and fell on top. It must have been rolled up in the shade. It resisted unfolding. It was brittle and yellow and kept rolling back to fit the roller. Susan unfolded the paper. On it someone had written *Go to the Room of the Eyes.*

Susan went down the hall to Kate's room.

"Look at this," she said. "I found it in my window shade."

"Go to the Room of the Eyes," read Kate. "That's funny, isn't it? It's like a clue in a treasure hunt. It's been there a long time, hasn't it?"

"I suppose the children who lived here were playing games," Susan said.

"If we knew which one was the Room of the Eyes we could look for another clue," Kate said.

"But it wouldn't still be there," Susan said.

"Why not? They never finished the game. If they had, they wouldn't have put this note back."

"Let's show Dave."

Dave pointed out that the Room of the Eyes could mean anything. "Look at the names we have for things," he said. "They could have called it that because two windows close together were like eyes, or because they used it to spy from, or it could be a pun, or a family joke."

"Well, that's all true," Susan said, "but I'm going to look around anyway."

"What do you care?" Kate said.

"I'd like to know about the people who lived here," Susan insisted. "I'm curious."

"Well, let's look around and see if we can find any eyes," Kate said.

"I might as well come along," Dave said.

They went through all the bedrooms on the second floor and looked in all the hall closets.

"There might be something at the back of the closet that would reflect and look like eyes," Dave said, flicking light switches.

They went up the winding stairs to the third floor. Here all was light and bright. The three little bedrooms had sloping ceilings, and doors opened from them onto the flat parts of the roof.

"I love these rooms," Kate said, "but I'd be afraid to sleep up here alone. Let's go out on the roof."

They stepped over the sill and out onto the tarred roof. It was like a little porch. Treetops waved near them and the peaked parts of the roof rose about them. You could climb up higher and go around the chimneys.

"We'd better keep Dinky away from here," Kate said. "That railing is awfully low and it's a long way down."

"Let's go in and look in the old ballroom," Susan said. The ballroom was so large that it had pillars down the middle to hold up the ceiling. It ran from the front of the house to the back, with windows floor to ceiling and French doors opening onto balconies. The doors had been sealed shut when the roofs were tarred. Even on this dark day and with the windows dirty, it was a lovely, light room, but woefully, sadly shabby. The paint was peeling, the plaster cracked, and the floor too rough for dancing now.

"It may have been a ballroom once," Susan said, "but it isn't anymore."

"Well, it'll make a swell playroom for Dinky and Jody," Dave said.

"No eyes here," Kate said. They looked in the closets under the eaves and found nothing.

"Would you like to sleep up here tonight, Dave?" Kate asked. "Mom wouldn't care. We could bring some cots and sleeping bags and sleep in one of the little rooms."

"Are you looking for ghosts?" Susan asked. "The realtor said these were maids' rooms. Maids wouldn't haunt a house, would they?"

"If we find the ghost of a maid, we'll capture her and give her to Mom," Dave said. "She could use one. I think it would be fun to sleep up here, and personally I'm glad we didn't find the Room of the Eyes. It's kind of a horrible idea, really."

"Well, I'm going to have breakfast and start on my room," Susan said. "I wish I had a hundred dollars to decorate my room with."

"I hate to go down," Kate said. "We're sure to have to work."

"Come down here, all of you," Mom called. "We've got a busy day. Kate, you've got to keep Dinky out from under my feet. Dave, this lawn is a mess. Start on it right after breakfast. May and I will do the grocery shopping and then May can bake. Now everybody try to think of things we have to get right away." We ate our breakfast and helped her with lists of things. We worked all day, except for a picnic in the park at noon. We even tried a little cleaning in the basement, but it was really too much. It had taken generations to accumulate all that junk. Surely, we told Mom, we couldn't be expected to undo the work of ages in a day.

"Well, you've got the dirt of the ages all over you," Mom said. "You all better have baths and we can have a quick supper and go to bed early. I'm exhausted."

We were all tired. By the time Dave and Kate got their cots and sleeping bags up to the third floor they were glad to crawl into them. Too sleepy even to read, they turned out the light and ate the candy bars Dave provided. The door onto the roof was open. The wind came up a little and the rain began to patter on the roof.

"Gosh, I'm glad you're here, Dave," Kate said.

"Me too," Dave said. "I mean, I'm glad you're here. It's a peaceful sound though, isn't it? It's sure quiet downstairs."

"Everyone's gone to sleep. Gosh, I hope we don't have to work so hard tomorrow."

"Me too."

They went to sleep. They must have slept for hours. They woke suddenly, at the same time. There was a noise on the roof. Their hearts came up in their mouths and they choked on them. Their blood sang in their veins with fear.

There were footsteps on the roof.

They could see, through the open door, the gray night sky. Then a shadow fell between them and the shape of a man stood there. Just a shape, a shadow. They shut their eyes in panic. There was a little stir, a wind — did he go past them? Did he go away, up, down, back the way he came? He must be on the roof, Dave thought. He went right by me, Kate thought, I know he did. There was a footstep, light as a falling leaf. With tight-shut eyes and beating hearts, they strained their ears and heard only the rain.

They waited — choking, cold, wet with fear. They waited a long time. There was nothing now but the soft wind and the falling rain. They got up and fled down the black winding stairway to Susan's room.

Kate turned on the light and they shook Susan awake. They were cold. Kate got into Susan's bed and Dave sat at the foot, wrapped in her spare blanket.

"What's the matter now?" Susan asked crossly. "If

this is going to happen every night, I'll have to get a bigger bed."

"Oh, Susan, hush up," Kate said. "There's a man upstairs."

"He came right up on the roof," Dave said.

"Sure," Susan said. "He comes knocking on a door three stories up in the air. Who is he, Dracula?"

"Dracula!" Dave gasped. "Golly, Sue, you don't think —"

"I think you're trying to scare me," Susan said. "Now get out of here and go to bed. I want to sleep."

"Scare you, for heaven's sake! We're scared to death ourselves. We were sound asleep and we heard this noise on the roof. He came right up to the door."

"You imagined it!" Susan said.

"No, we didn't."

"And then he vanished, I suppose," Susan said.

"I think he went into the ballroom," Kate said.

"I don't," Dave said. "I think he's on the roof. I think he's still up there. He may be in the ballroom by now, though. Should we get Dad?"

"No, of course not. You're just crazy, you two," Susan said. "You can't even agree on what happened."

Well, after all, Susan's word was law. She was the eldest and she always decided. She said we imagined it and that we shouldn't tell Dad, and of course we would go along with that. Besides, if there was a man (and we were not so sure, now) then there was a mystery, and it was our mystery, not Dad's. Dad would be sure to spoil it. Anyway, Susan was taking over now.

"Come on," Susan said. "I'll go up there with you. Now where did I put my flashlight?"

"There are lights, you know," Dave said.

"I don't know if there are any bulbs in the ballroom sockets," Susan said. "Come on."

"Gosh, you're brave," Kate said. "How about if I just stay down here?"

"On your feet," Dave said. "None of that. All of us or none."

"I wish it was none," Kate said.

"All right, follow me, you scaredy-cats," Susan said. She led the way into the hall, clicking on light switches. It was amazing how much braver Dave and Kate felt, with Susan's sturdy figure striding ahead of them and the stairs ablaze with lights.

They went upstairs and turned on the lights in the room where they had slept. Empty. Only their cots and the open door. They didn't like to look at the door.

They went on to the ballroom.

"Where are the lights?" Susan whispered.

"I don't know."

They peered into the vast blackness. The gray windows cast a little light onto the near bare floor, but the middle was an awful formless shadow. Susan reached around the door and felt for the light switch.

"Look," Dave whispered.

"Where? Oh, my gosh!" Kate moaned.

"Where?" Susan said.

"Right in the middle," Kate said. "Eyes."

Two horrid round eyes, unwinking, unmoving, shone out of the black shadow.

Susan found the light switch and turned it on.

"What is it?" she asked. "Over here? It looks like a dead cat or something." She went bravely toward it.

"Susan, are you crazy or something?" Dave asked. "He may be here, anywhere."

"Oh, pooh," Susan said. "Look here, kids, it's a teddy bear, some little kid's teddy bear. No, it's not either, it's a gingerbread man. I've never seen anything quite like it. It looks just like a real gingerbread man." She held up a stuffed toy, good-sized, made out of brown plush with pink velvet stripes, imitating icing, and a pleasant, open, raisiny expression.

"Is that all?" Dave said. "Well, let's look around."

They looked around, but in that bare room it didn't take long. They even, with great courage, looked into the closets under the eaves.

"I told you you imagined it," Susan said.

"Why didn't we see the gingerbread man this morning?" Kate said. "We couldn't have missed it."

"We did miss it, though," Dave said. "Let's take our cots and sleeping bags, Kate, and sleep in Susan's room."

"What, again?" Susan said. "I thought I was supposed to have a room of my own. I'm glad we found gingerbread man anyway. We can give him to Dinky tomorrow. She'll love him."

"Maybe he went back out," Dave said.

"And climbed down three stories in the rain?" Kate said.

"Well, either that or he's still up there someplace," Dave persisted.

"Oh, let's go to sleep," Susan said. "He never was there at all and you know it."

"Listen, Susan," Kate said, "do you think that's the Room of the Eyes? Where the gingerbread man was?"

"I never thought of it," Susan said. "How could they know he'd always be there?"

"Maybe the Room of the Eyes is wherever he is," Dave suggested.

"Oh, let's go to sleep," Susan said.

»»»»» 5 «««««

Jody woke suddenly and all together, as he always did. For anyone who slept as soundly as he did — you could pick him up and carry him around and he never knew it — he could wake up very efficiently. He stretched his bones and knobby muscles. Then he doubled up his sharp knees and elbows and stretched again. He looked around his room with pleasure. It was about as full as a room could get and looked as though it had been stirred with a stick, but each item was useful in its way. All the books he had inherited from the rest of us he kept untidily in two bookshelves which overflowed onto the floor. There were books under his bed and on his patchwork quilt. Pinned on his bulletin board were several drawings of rockets, because he was interested in rockets just now, and scattered on his bed and on the floor were sheets from the calendar he had been making when he fell asleep. Jody was only seven, but he had so many intellectual interests that it was hard for the rest of us to bear. We wished he were more normal.

Jody jumped out of bed and stretched some more. Then he spent a little time looking affectionately at his collection shelf. On it were a large jar of corn silk, a great many shells, a jar of buttons, and a box of orange seeds, in case he should want to be a farmer someday. Jody stepped over the train and the blocks on the floor. If he kept them up in the old ballroom as he was supposed to do, how could he play with them in the middle of the night?

Then he went to the window, opened it very wide, and leaned way out. A soft drizzle of rain touched his cheek. He looked out at the Space Needle. He'd first seen it years before, when he was very small. It had just been built for the Fair then. They came into Seattle for the World's Fair and Dad had taken him up in the elevator to see the view. There was a huge steel framework, like the Eiffel Tower, and on top of it a restaurant that spun slowly round and round, like the earth. This magical thing could be seen from his window and he looked for it the first thing each morning. There it was now, clear on the horizon and looking like a tomato on the end of a fork. He loved to watch it, but he wished he could see it turning round. What if it got going faster and faster? What if it lifted right off and sailed away, like a spaceship?

All those people eating breakfast in the restaurant would be surprised!

"Jody, Jody," May was calling, "come down for breakfast right away."

"Why?" he asked reasonably. "It's still vacation, isn't it?"

"Mom wants you," May said. "She wants us all. I don't know why."

Jody got his ski sweater out of the closet and put it on over his pajamas. He liked to wear ski clothes as much as possible, even in the summer. Tastefully attired in this way, he started downstairs. Funny how big the front stairs had looked when he first saw them. Now they seemed to have shrunk, but doubtless he himself had grown in the week or so we had been here. He slid down the banister and ran into the kitchen.

The rest of us were already there. Dave, looking sleepy but interested, was watching Mom frying bacon and sausage.

"Gosh, Mom," he said, "what's happening? Is inflation over? Where's the economy-sized box of oatmeal?"

"No, indeed," Mom said, "prices are going up all the time. I'm defrosting the icebox and I've got part of a package of this and part of that and I'm cooking up the whole thing."

"Is that why you got us up?" May asked. "Just to eat up the leftovers?"

"No, I've got a project for today," Mom said.

"If it's cleaning the basement," Dave said, "I refuse."

"It's not the basement," Mom said. "Now eat a good breakfast, children, and finish everything up. The weather is supposed to improve. In fact, it's going to clear. We'll have a lovely summer morning painting pictures."

"Painting pictures!" Susan said. "Why, I haven't painted since I was in kindergarten."

"And I almost flunked kindergarten," Kate said, "because I couldn't paint. If I hadn't known that math was coming I never would have stuck it out."

"I can paint," Jody said. "I'll make you some rockets, Mom."

"I don't want rockets," Mom said. "I want some big, splashy, wild paintings for the front hall. Abstractions. That dark hall is driving me mad. I got some frames at the Goodwill yesterday and we'll just fill them up."

"There it goes," Jody said. "I thought it would fly off sometime."

"What is it, Jody?" Susan said. "What's flying off?"

"The top of the Space Needle," Jody said. "It just spun faster and faster and then off it went and now those people in the restaurant are going to Mars or someplace."

"That's just a plane, Jody," Dave said. "Don't be so dumb. Nothing can happen to the Space Needle."

"I see it," Dinky said. She always saw everything Jody did.

"It's an interesting idea," Mom said, "but luckily I think you're mistaken." Like a lot of Jody's ideas, silly as it was it stayed in our minds, and it wasn't hard to imagine the whole lighted top, like a magic observation car, sailing through the clouds.

"I just remembered," Mom said. "Your father has a visiting specialist of some kind to take around today and they were having breakfast at the Space Needle."

"Now don't worry, Mom," Jody said. "I must have been mistaken. If Dad is there, nothing will happen. He wouldn't stand for it."

"I was mistaken too," Dinky said.

We all knew, except Dinky, that when you're seven you can believe two things at once. Just last Christmas, Jody had told us all over and over that there was no Santa Claus, but after Christmas he wrote him a thank-you note, which is more than he did for Grandma. S. Claus, North Pole, and an airmail stamp.

"See," Mom said when we had finished the leftovers, "the sky is growing lighter already. If you girls will pick up the dishes, I'll go out and set up the easels."

"Easels!" May said. "We don't have any easels."

"Mom probably found them in the basement," Jody said. "There's everything you can think of down there."

When we finished the dishes and went to find Mom she had set up three stepladders on the back porch. She had tacked big pieces of cardboard on the slanting sides so that they were like double easels.

"Are we going to paint on that old cardboard?" May asked. "Our hall is going to look pretty funny with a lot of pieces of cardboard hanging around."

"I've got these old window shades," Mom said. "I found them in one of the upstairs closets. Just thumbtack whatever size piece you want onto the cardboard. They're pretty much like canvas. Now, I've got chalks — pastels, that is — and poster paints and watercolors and finger paints, or you might melt color crayons."

"Melt color crayons!" Dave said. "Mom, you don't seem to know anything about art."

"I'm not asking for art," Mom said, "just a lot of lovely color."

"Okay," Susan said, "here goes." She started tacking up her window shade. The rest of us followed suit. Susan took the pastels, because she liked to rub them together and see what happened.

The thing about painting a picture, even a lousy one, is that by the time you get yourself dreamed into it (because even an abstraction has to have an idea), the whole world looks different and you can see things that are usually invisible. Shadows, ordinarily gray, become colored. The park behind the house, where we looked for inspiration, broke into many greens, and this green upon green was patterned in points and pillars of light. Mom wanted abstractions, and none of us could draw anyway, but we found ourselves trying very hard to make the color look like what the sky and the grass and the trees made us think of. We said we couldn't paint, and we can't, but of course we love to do it, just as we surreptitiously and with little skill write poetry and keep diaries, because it's so exciting, like running a race. You can't think about anything else and you enjoy every minute of it and yet you long and long to be through. The best moment is when you've just finished and you still think it's good.

We painted furiously, once we got started, and the time must have passed in an unusual way, because suddenly Mom was saying, "Well, I've finished the fridge and most of the pantry and wiped up the kitchen floor. You've been at it two hours. Let's see what you've done."

We all fell back and looked at our canvases. Then we looked at each other's.

"Not bad," Mom was saying. "It just shows you, aimlessly splashing watercolor can give you something interesting."

"But it wasn't aimless, Mom," Dave said. "I had a very definite idea."

"You did?" Mom said. "What was it?"

"If you can't tell," Dave said angrily, "I'm not going to point it out."

"Why, you're acting like an artist," Mom said, "temperamental."

There was no use telling her that for a few minutes we had all felt like artists. Probably temperament goes with it.

"What have you been doing, Dinky?" Mom said.

"This is an eagle," Dinky said proudly, pointing to something that looked more like an amoeba.

"It doesn't look much like one," Jody said.

"I believe that a witch has eaten part of it," Dinky said.

"Look at mine," Jody said. "It's a rainbow from inside." We all looked. It was remarkable. The colors seemed to surround us. Jody's powerful imagination had gotten into the picture and it made you feel like a moth in a chandelier.

"What made you think of a rainbow?" Mom asked.

"And why from the inside?" Susan asked.

"Why, it's rainbow weather," Jody said. "I expect one any minute. It's been raining and the sun is coming and going."

"I don't feel a rainbow coming on," Kate said.

"Well, I do," Jody said. "I'll bet if we go out in the front yard and look all around we'll see one." He ran around the side of the house. "There it is!" he called back. We all went and looked.

"Gosh, what a beauty!" Dave said. There it was, as perfect as possible, a great striped ribbon of color that stretched right across the valley.

"You could walk over it and come down in Queen Anne," Susan said.

"You can't walk on a rainbow," Jody said learnedly. "It's just refracted light."

"All right, you little smart aleck," Dave said, "what about the pot of gold?"

"What pot of gold?" Jody said.

"Don't you know there's a pot of gold at the end of the rainbow?" Dave asked. "Here you read all these books about dinosaurs and planets, but you don't even know about the pot of gold."

"Don't tease him," Susan said. "It's just a story, Jody. There's supposed to be a pot of gold at the end of the rainbow."

"Then why don't we go get it?" Jody asked. He was at it again, believing two things at once.

"It's very hard to find the end of the rainbow," Susan said.

"But I can see it," Jody said. "I can see it right over there. I'm going."

"Come back here," Mom said, "and put some pants on. You can't go over there in your pajamas. If he wants to look for that rainbow, you better take him, Susan. He can't cross all those streets by himself."

"It'll only last a minute anyway," Susan said.

But when Jody came back with his pants on, the rainbow was still there, stretching from Capitol Hill to Queen Anne Hill.

"Come on, Susan," Jody said, "hurry up!"

They ran up to the corner. "Down there!" Jody cried, and they ran down the next block.

"Wait, Jody, you can't cross Tenth alone," Susan said.

"If we're in the crosswalk, the cars have to stop," Jody said.

"Not when they're going this fast," Susan said firmly. She grabbed his arm and held him back.

"Now!" she said, and they raced across the street.

"It's up there," Jody cried, "by that castle."

"That's not a castle," Susan said. "That's the Cathedral."

"It looks like a castle to me," Jody said. "Look at the big front door."

They ran up the long walk to the Cathedral steps.

"It's around behind," Jody said.

"It's fading, Jody," Susan said. "I'm afraid the rainbow's going away."

"It doesn't want us to find the pot of gold," Jody panted. "It knows we're hot on its trail. My, this is a big castle."

Behind the Cathedral the land drops so precipitately that nothing can be built there, and there is a wilderness of crooked trees and wild blackberry. Elsewhere on the west side of Capitol Hill the slope is more gradual, and there are old farmhouses with apple trees and gardens, and little Japanese houses and artists' studios. Here it was steep and wild and empty, like a piece of Mt. Rainier right in town.

When they reached the back of the Cathedral the rainbow was lifting and thinning. There was just the ghost of a rainbow left and it was across the valley.

"This is where it was," Jody said, and plunged down over the edge.

"Come back, Jody," Susan said. "You can't go down there. You'll fall."

"I can't fall," Jody said. "I'm stuck in the wild blackberry."

"Well, I'm coming," Susan said. "I'll get you out, but I don't see why you had to go down there anyway."

"To see if the pot of gold is still there," Jody said reasonably. "Hurry up and come down here. I think I can see something."

"Now I'm stuck," Susan said, pulling blackberry from her sweater. "They're all wound around my legs and I'm sopping wet."

"Look down there, Susan," Jody said. "I can see it, I'm sure I can." He hopped up and down in excitement and some of the vines holding him came loose. He slid very rapidly a few feet down the hill and fell.

"Where are you?" Susan asked crossly. "I can't see you. If you're not careful, you'll go over the edge of a cliff or something."

"I've got it," Jody cried, "I've almost got it. Come on and see!"

Susan got loose at last and crept a few feet closer to Jody.

"What do you see?" she asked. "I don't see anything."

"It's right there, under that bush, can't you see?"

There was something shiny under the bush. They strained toward it.

"I've got it," Jody said, "but it's empty. It's a pretty pot, though. Do you suppose it spilled?"

Susan slid a few more feet and slipped down beside him.

"There's something else too," Jody said. He groped around in the brush and brought out a gold candlestick.

"My goodness, Jody," Susan said, "this hasn't anything to do with the rainbow. You knew that was just a story, didn't you? I think these things must belong to the Cathedral."

"You mean there never was any gold in this? You mean it's just like the Easter Bunny? Just a story?"

"I'm afraid so," Susan said.

"Maybe the pot of gold is at the other end, over on that other hill," Jody said.

"Anyway it's too late now," Susan said, "because the rainbow isn't in Queen Anne either and it's beginning to rain. We better find someone at the Cathedral and give them these things. Fish around and see if you can find another candlestick." Jody found another candlestick and another vase too. They crept back up the prickly slope, getting wetter than ever.

"You see," Jody said, as they crossed the parking lot, "here are the places where the knights have their horses. This must be a castle. Look, there are their names."

"Oh, Jody," Susan said tiredly, "let's not pretend anymore. That's where the clergymen park their cars. That doesn't say Sir Percival or Sir Launcelot, does it? It says Mr. Michelson."

They went around to the front, carrying their loot.

"I feel kind of guilty," Susan said. "What if they think we stole these?" They pushed through one of the big doors and stood in the vast empty nave.

"Goodness, I feel funny, don't you?" Jody whispered. "It's awful big, isn't it, and high?"

"There's an old man down there by the altar," Susan said. "Let's go down there."

They started down the aisle. It was miles long. The old gentleman stood with his back to them. He wore a long black robe and his silver hair came down to his collar.

"I believe it's Merlin," Jody whispered.

"Hush up," Susan hissed.

"Please, sir," she began timidly. The old gentleman turned around.

"Please, we found these. . . ."

42

"You have them! You found them!" the man said in a high trembling voice. "Oh, praise heaven, they are returned!" He took the gold vessels and the candlesticks and almost ran up to the altar with them.

"Well," Susan said, "I guess there's no doubt about where they belong."

"He seemed happy, didn't he?" Jody said.

The old man came back. His wrinkled face was lighted with happiness and he smiled and smiled.

"They were stolen last night," he said. "We will let the police know that they have been found. Now you must tell me what happened."

"They were at the foot of the rainbow," Jody said, "but the rainbow moved its feet and there wasn't any gold so we thought we must have made a mistake."

"Can you make this any clearer?" the old gentleman asked Susan. "Was there a rainbow?"

"Yes, it was a beautiful rainbow and we were telling Jody about the pot of gold at the end of the rainbow and he wanted to look for it and we found these things instead," Susan said.

"I see," he said. "Yes, I see, the sign in the sky. Do you believe in miracles?"

"Well, sometimes," Susan said hesitantly.

"I do," Jody said. "Say, are you Merlin?"

"I? Merlin?" the old gentleman asked. "No, I am not Merlin. I am Canon Michelson. Who are you? Robin Goodfellow?"

44

"I'm Jody Evans and this is Susan Evans. She's my sister," Jody said.

"I am very happy to know you," Canon Michelson said, "and if your name is Evans, I believe I know where you live. You just moved in, I believe?"

"Yes, we did," Susan said.

"Some of my dearest memories," he said, "are associated with that house. Dear me, what wonderful times we used to have. I used to play there, you know, when I was a little boy. There used to be a game that started, *Go to the Room of the Eyes.* My, my, that's a long time ago, long ago. And they're all gone now, you know, all those happy children."

He looked very sad suddenly, and Susan, though she longed to ask him about the room with the eyes, did not dare.

"We'd better go now," she said.

"Accept our heartfelt thanks," Canon Michelson said gravely, "and tell your mother I will call on her."

When we got home Mom was tacking the paintings that were dry into the frames she had gotten from the Goodwill. It's amazing how just putting a frame on a picture makes it look professional. Susan's dreaming greens and the strange yellow picture Dave had made, like sun soaking into the earth, looked natural and lovely in the ornate gold frames. It made us wonder. Perhaps everyone paints his own pictures!

"Well, did you find the pot of gold?" Mom asked.

45

"Yes, but it was empty so we gave it to the man at the castle," Jody said.

"Someone had stolen the gold service off the Cathedral altar, Mom," Susan said. "It was stolen last night and then I guess they just threw it down the hill. It was right where the rainbow was. Canon Michelson said it was a miracle."

"They stole from the church!" Mom said in a shocked voice. "How terrible. Who would do a thing like that? Why would anyone do it?"

"For kicks, Mom. Lots of kids do things like that for kicks," Dave said.

"What kind of a word is that? Kicks! How silly. I can't believe it."

"Just the same," Dave said, "I'll bet that's all it was. They didn't keep them, did they? All right, they did it for kicks."

"God was mad," Jody said gravely. "He was very angry because someone stole His dishes and He pointed the rainbow at them so He could get them back."

"Listen, Mom," Susan said, "Canon Michelson used to know the people who lived here. He's coming to call and you must be sure to ask him about the Room of the Eyes."

"Room of the Eyes!" Mom said. "This is too much. First the Space Needle floats away, then we have a rainbow and a miracle. No, it's too much. I'll be glad when school starts."

>>>>>> **6** <<<<<<

SCHOOL STARTED, and our cold rainy summer disappeared. The sun came out, the cloud and mist disappeared, you could see for miles; out of hiding came the mountains and the Sound. Mt. Rainier, which had been brooding behind a cloud all summer, now came close and clear and hovered over us. The Olympics leaped up on one side and the Cascades sprang to life on the other. The laughing, sparkling blue water appeared as if by magic. It was hot.

The streets were full of children in school uniforms. In the city, we learned, a lot of children go to parochial schools and a lot of them go to private schools. There were red plaid jumpers, blue plaid jumpers, green pleated skirts, middy blouses. What makes a uniform look like a uniform anyway? You can always tell. Susan went to private school and had

47

a navy blue uniform, wool and very warm, and lots of homework. This was not as bad as it might have been, she said, because the girls at school were all in the same boat, all very hot in their wool uniforms and all tired from their homework. About ten at night they called each other up and felt sorry for each other. The rest of us, except Dinky, went to public school. We did not have uniforms, but we had new school clothes which were also very warm.

"Why don't you wear summer dresses?" Mom asked. "And Jody could wear shorts." But of course we couldn't do that.

Dinky played around all day by herself, very cool and comfortable in a sunsuit, and cried a good deal because she couldn't go to school. She had grown very fond of the plush gingerbread boy and carried him around with her. Jody felt bad because he didn't have any homework and the rest of us felt bad because we did.

Ever since we started keeping up with Russia, homework has been getting worse. Parents are anxious for their children to work hard and learn to cope with the complexity of modern life, and teachers cooperate by giving us fifty problems instead of twenty-five. The strange thing is that adults themselves are always striking for shorter working hours and writing articles giving advice on how to cope with greater leisure.

That is one of the things that we think about a lot

and it is too bad no one ever asks us to write a theme about it.

What we are writing about now, though, is the first day of school.

Jody was going into second grade, and because he was new at the school he had to stand in line for a long time, waiting to be assigned to a room. He was hungry because of not being able to eat breakfast (his throat was choked up, he explained, and felt as though nerves had grown across it) and very tired of standing in line. Finally he went in one of the rooms and got an encyclopedia and sat on the floor and read it. As a consequence, he was dragged off to be tested the very first day. Usually we are at school several days before they begin testing us. The testing lady made him read for her and then she asked him questions for hours. Finally Jody said he couldn't stand it anymore. He opened his lunch pail and told her if she would stop asking him questions she could have his dessert. Evidently she felt sorry for him then because she told him to eat his lunch and then she would take him to his classroom. It turned out to be a special class where they take second and third grades in one year. It had a binocular microscope and a tape recorder and an aquarium and a TV and some hamsters and rabbits, and they can learn Spanish from tapes. It looks as though Jody is going to be very happy because he doesn't care about people much.

May sat next to a Chinese girl. After about ten minutes' talk and a quick look at the girl's neat papers and handwriting, May knew, with sinking heart, that she had met her match and that this girl was smarter than she. But years of living with five brothers and sisters had made May rather clever about getting along; she was so glad to find someone who read the same books she did that inside of an hour they were friends forever.

May and Jody were, in their own ways, all right. But for Kate and Dave the first day was one long agony and they still cannot look back without a shrinking feeling. Never before had they been without friends. Never before had they been without each other. This school was big enough to have two sixth grades and being twins, they were sent to different rooms.

One thing, Kate thought, as she sat at the unfamiliar desk and looked about her at the alien faces, at least all schools smell the same. If she shut her eyes she would be aware only of the homelike smell of chalk, people, and disinfectant, hear only a babble of voices and echoes from the hall outside. But open them she must. What a variety of children there were! It was like the United Nations. There were Indians from India and a new boy from Peru, let alone such American types as Japanese, Chinese, and Negro. There were white children who looked very poor and one at least who looked very rich. That smooth-haired girl in the dark green kilt and knee socks, she had that air imparted indefinably by a privileged childhood. One knew, immediately, that she didn't run around looking for clean socks in the morning or eat a breakfast served by a sleepy mother in a bathrobe. She would come from a well-ordered house with top drawers full of socks and a cook in the kitchen. Some of these children looked as though they'd had no breakfast at all.

"Now, class," the teacher said, "in your best handwriting, write a short paragraph on 'My Summer Vacation.' Head your papers this way," and she wrote, in flowing script, on the blackboard, *Name, class, date.*

Kate raised her hand.

"Does it have to be script?" she asked. "Can't we print?"

"Print!" the teacher said in an awful voice.

"Yes, in my other school we printed."

"You mean you're in the sixth grade and you don't know how to write?" the teacher said. Everyone looked at Kate and laughed. The whole class laughed at her.

"It's time you learned," the teacher said in a slightly kinder voice.

"Where did you go to school before?" the girl behind Kate whispered. Kate whispered back and told her.

"Where do you live now?"

Kate told her.

"You mean that big brown run-down place? It's haunted, isn't it?"

Kate turned right around and said, "It is not!"

"Katherine Evans!" the teacher said. "I don't know what they taught you at that other school, but here, at this school, we don't talk during class!" Kate knew her face was red as fire. She bent over her paper and tried to write.

"I know it's haunted," the voice behind her continued, "because I have a friend who lived over near there and she says it's been empty for ever so long and there are lights moving around in it at night."

Kate went on writing.

"I live in an apartment," the voice went on. "It's a beautiful new apartment house and my mother is president of the PTA."

Kate finished her paper without talking and the voice behind her gave up finally and started whispering to someone else. She got through arithmetic all right, she was good at that, and it cheered her up a little. Then it was time for recess.

All of a sudden it seemed to her that she had to do something to make an impression on somebody. She had to make friends with someone, somehow, and be noticed and liked again. It was almost as though another person took charge and pushed her restlessly from group to group, talking in a silly, over-friendly way, gabbling really, while her real self watched helplessly. Even while she said to herself, Don't try so hard, calm down, Kate, take it easy, still she went rushing nervously here and there.

"Come on, everybody," someone called, "here's the balls. Let's play squares."

A ball came rolling Kate's way. She picked it up.

"Here, give me that ball!" A long-legged, mean-looking Negro girl grabbed at the ball. "You don't know how to play, white girl!" She glared crossly at Kate and knocked the ball from Kate's hand. She gave Kate a great shove and grabbed the bouncing ball. Kate fell down, but she was up again in a minute. She was blazing mad and she slapped the Negro girl.

"Katherine! Katherine Evans!" The teacher was there in an instant. She grabbed Kate by the arm and dragged her over to the corner of the playground.

"We don't allow fighting here," she said, "and I am especially angry because you attacked Linda, who is one of our transfers. She's here from another school as our guest. You must always be especially kind to Negroes because they have been badly treated in the past. Just because Linda belongs to a minority group don't think you can mistreat her here!"

How to explain, Kate thought dazedly, that she hadn't hit Linda because she was a Negro, but because she took the ball? That she hadn't even noticed, or had been too mad to care, what color Linda was — that she, Kate, was very kindhearted and hadn't hit anyone outside her own family for years — that she was nervous and lost her temper and was new here too. She rubbed her bruised elbow and said nothing.

"Now go and sit in the classroom," the teacher finished.

The rest of the day passed in a kind of painful blur, and finally Kate found herself walking home with Dave. Dave had a black eye.

"How'd it go?" he asked.

"Awful," Kate said. Only to Dave, because he was her twin, would she have thought of recounting her humiliating experiences.

"I can't see why I acted like I did," she said hopelessly when she had told about her terrible day. "I just felt I had to make people notice me."

"Sounds as though they noticed you all right," Dave said, "but I know what you mean. I know that when you're new you should just sit back and keep your mouth shut and especially not brag or talk much, but you can't help it."

"Is that how you got your black eye?"

"I'll tell you about that later," Dave said gruffly.

Kate tried to tell him about Linda.

"She really is mean," she said. "She was rude to everyone, even the teacher. She's so nasty you forget she's Negro."

"You mean you can hate her for herself alone?" Dave asked.

"Doesn't that sound awful?" Kate laughed and

began to feel more like herself. "You know what I mean. Look how nice Negroes usually are. When Negroes are mean you forget they're Negroes and you forget to be especially nice and you get just as mad at them as if they were white."

"I've got to learn handwriting too," Dave said.

"Jody's probably got a book about it," Kate said. "We can practice."

After a while Dave said, "I did just what you did. I went around like a fool, trying to be friendly. Finally, I couldn't think of much to say so I told this guy about Jody finding the candlesticks and things at the foot of the rainbow."

"I don't see anything wrong with that," Kate said.

"So he didn't say anything at all. He went over and talked to another guy and this guy came over to me and he said, 'Wise guy, eh? Look at the little wise guy!' and he hit me."

"What for?" Kate asked.

"Well, I suppose he was the one who stole the things from the church, don't you think? They probably thought I knew they did it. So now I've got enemies and I don't even know anyone yet."

"They'll forget about it, won't they?" Kate asked. "Now that he's hit you, he'll probably forget all about it."

"I don't think so," Dave said. "I think I'm in for trouble."

"Did you hear anything about our house? Being haunted, I mean?"

"Yes, I heard that too."

Haunted or not, it was nice to be home again. Dinky came out and hugged them both.

"I had a terrible day," she said, "all by myself, and then a man tried to steal my gingerbread man."

"Oh, Dinky," Kate said, "that's not true, is it?"

"Yes, it is," Dinky said, "but I ran away. We're going to have supper on the porch because it's so hot."

It was like summer in the Midwest, eating on the porch at Grandma's, but the instant the sun went down it got very cold. Dad built a fire in the living-room fireplace and we all lay down in front of it. Dinky was so glad to have everyone home that she kept cuddling up to us all in turn and finally settled down with her head in Susan's lap and her feet in Kate's. She held her gingerbread boy and beamed around at everyone.

"I like to be all scrunched together like this," she said.

"Dinky would like us to be like frogs' eggs," Dave said, "all plastered together in a kind of jelly."

"Well, it's getting late," Dad said. "Homework time. You'll have to break out of your jelly and strike out to the open sea."

7

THE HOT WEATHER held, except for the usual drizzle over the weekend. Early Monday morning fog gave way to blue skies, and by the time we started to school the sun was blazing down. It was football weather. It was the time of year when, at our other house, we played games after supper every night. School had been going for a week and had not improved particularly. Kate and Dave walked home from school together.

"Let's go up in the park," Kate said. "It's such a nice day and I haven't anything to do."

"I haven't either. I wish I had someone to play football with," Dave said. "I don't know many of the guys yet."

"I don't either," Katie said. "I don't know anybody much either."

"You must know the girls in your class," Dave said.

"Sort of," Kate said, "but all they do is ask me about my haunted house and they don't seem very anxious to play with me."

"I hear about that too," Dave said. "I guess we've just started off on the wrong foot."

"We're not good at moving, that's all," Kate said. "Gosh, some kids in my class move all the time. They're used to going to a couple of schools a year and they're always changing apartments. I don't see how they stand it."

"Me neither," Dave said. "You know what, Kate, we're homesick. It just comes over me in waves. I feel sick to my stomach."

"I know," Kate said. "I almost cried today in school." They sat down on the dry grass and looked about them at the park's trees and flowers and the incredible view of Sound and mountains.

"Sure is pretty here," Kate said.

"Sure is," Dave said listlessly.

"I've got a lot of homework," Kate said.

"So have I," Dave said. "I'll bet I've got more than you have. And that's something that's going to get worse. Next year I'll be in junior high and Mom and Dad will expect me to get in the honors classes."

"I'll bet you'll have to go to private school, like Susan," Kate said. "I think that's why we moved over here, so they could send us to those terrible tough schools so we can go to the kind of college that's hard to get into."

"I can always flunk the entrance exams," Dave said.

"I'm not exactly sorry we moved," Kate said. "I like the house and all. I suppose we'll get used to it."

"I like the house too, but I haven't felt the same since we saw that man. Do you think we imagined that?" Dave asked.

"Of course not!" Kate said. "How could we have imagined it together? What I want to know is where he went. And I don't like this Room of the Eyes business either. It gives me the willies."

"Funny, in stories it always sounds like fun to live in a house with a mystery, but in real life it isn't much fun. It makes it seem as if it wasn't our house somehow," Dave said.

"I'm getting hungry," Kate said.

"Gosh, yes," Dave said.

They got up and walked slowly down the hill and through the woods. As they came down the last steep incline they could see their house.

"It looks funny from above," Dave said, "all those little roofs and peaks and chimneys."

"I never thought I'd live in a house with four chimneys," Kate said.

"There's someone on a ladder," Dave said. "Wonder who it is?"

"Must be the window washer," Kate said. "Mom

said someone was coming to do the outside of the windows. I suppose we'll have to do the inside."

They crossed the untidy back yard and went in at the back door.

"Hi, who's that?" Mom called.

"Just us," Dave said. "Kate and me."

"Well, come on in the kitchen," Mom said. "There's a new box of apples. May and I are making doughnuts."

"Is that man going to wash all the windows?" Kate asked.

"Yes," Mom said. "We won't be able to afford it all the time, but I wanted them clean to start with anyway. Guess how many windows there are."

"Seventy-five," Kate said.

"Two hundred," Dave said.

"No, there's an even hundred, counting the doors with glass in them. Isn't that a lot? But I counted them myself and I only got ninety-nine. But as I told the man, I won't quibble over one window. I'm always making mistakes like that."

"Of course you know what that means, don't you, Mom?" Dave said. "You've read all the books about counting windows, haven't you? I suppose we'd better count them, Kate."

"What for?" Kate said.

"I know," May said wisely. "Just don't prick your finger on a spindle."

"What are you children talking about?" Mom said.

"If you're thinking of a secret room, you're crazy. We've been all over this place. You read too many books. It's easy to make a mistake counting windows. Have some doughnuts instead." They took some doughnuts and then Mom said, "How's school? How come you don't bring any kids home? Our house used to be full of kids."

"Oh, never mind, Mom," Kate said. "Let's go count windows, Dave."

They went outside and began to count.

"There's no use in our counting together," Dave said. "You go inside and count and I'll count outside and we'll see if we get the same."

So Kate went inside and wandered around counting.

"He would make me walk up and down all these stairs," she said to herself. She was all alone on the basement stairs and she thought she might as well cry a little. Sometimes crying made you feel better. She walked around with the tears running down her face and counted the dusty windows. Camping room, wood room, furnace room, kindling room, laundry, hall, bathroom, storerooms, then the big room. Someday it would be fun to come down here and really go through all this stuff. There was a black book press on the shelf, and an ancient Victorian coatrack. There was a lot of old porch furniture, a rocking chair, a plant stand . . .

"Hey, Kate," Dave called, "what are you doing? A hundred is right. Mom is wrong."

"Well, you're wrong," Kate said. "I only got ninety-nine."

"Let's do it again," Dave said.

"I don't want to do it again," Kate said. "I'm going up to my room."

"Oh, come on, Kate, it's better to do something," Dave said.

"I don't think so," Kate said. She went upstairs and changed into cut-offs and a shirt. Then she lay down on her bed and felt sorry for herself.

Dave went in the kitchen and ate some doughnuts.

"If you eat so many doughnuts you'll get fat," May said. "You're just the right age to get pre-adolescent fat."

"Where did you get that?"

"Out of that *Children from Ten to Sixteen* book," May said.

"Listen," Dave said, "why don't you read about your own age? Find out how repulsive it is. Why do you keep cooking all the time if you don't want me to eat?"

"Because I haven't anything else to do and anyway I love to cook. Who was right about the windows?"

"We have ninety-nine on the inside and one hundred on the outside," Dave said.

"Well, where's the extra window?" May said.

"I don't know."

"Well, you should know. Don't you ever read any books? You can put a lighted candle in each window and then look around outside and see which window has no candle and that's the room where the crazy uncle or whatever-it-is is kept."

"I can see myself getting a hundred candles," Dave said.

"Or," May went on, "one of you can go around on the inside and one on the outside and you look at each other from each window and when you miss one you know. Did you do it that way? Because if you didn't —"

"All right, May, all right," Dave said. "I get the picture." He went up to Kate's room.

"Come on, Kate," he said, "this is vital. Now let's count the windows again. You on one side and me on the other."

"I don't want to find a secret room," Kate said. "We've got troubles enough." Then she said, "Oh, all right."

Kate stayed inside and Dave went outside and together they paced the house. Kate passed from room to room and floor to floor. Her face, growing smaller and less distinct as she ascended, peered at Dave from one window after another. Ninety-nine at last.

"Where's the other one?" Kate called.

"Come down here," Dave said. "I'll show you."

"There it is," he said when they stood on the lawn, "up in that highest gable."

63

"There must be an attic after all," Kate said. "You know Dad went up the trapdoor and said there was nothing but insulation."

"Part of it must be closed off and he didn't realize it," Dave said. "Let's go up on the roof and see."

"But I heard the man go through the ballroom."

"I didn't. You were so scared you don't know what you heard. I think he went up on the roof. Let's look anyway."

"I've been going up and down these stairs all day," Kate said.

"Good for the legs," Dave said. "Good training for skiing."

They went through the little room where they had slept that night and out onto the flat roof, then climbed one of the little gables, circled the chimney, and came out onto a great flat expanse of tarred roof.

"Gosh, it's like a parking lot," Kate said.

It was like being on a mountaintop. The wind had a clear sweep, and they felt close to the sun. They felt strangely bold and free and also (a feeling which has come to us when we were visiting on the prairie) strangely exposed. There was nothing to hide behind. There they were, walking along the skyline, and plain for all the world to see.

"Should we get down and creep?" Kate said.

"Don't be silly," Dave said. "There's nothing to be afraid of, is there?"

"My goodness, I don't know," Kate said. "Danger may be lurking anywhere."

"There's no place for it to lurk," Dave said.

"What's that box thing over there?"

"That's the trapdoor cover, but it's nowhere near the window. Let's look over at that gable first. If we don't find anything we can come back and go down that trap, but it'll be dark and we didn't bring any flashlights."

They walked slowly across the roof toward the gable with the window in it.

"What are you going to do if you find a secret room?" Kate asked.

"Well, if it's just a room with nothing in it we can use it for meetings or something, but if he's there — that is, if we find a door and open it and he's sitting there, well, I don't know. . . ."

They came to the edge of the tar, where the shingled part of the roof rose in low peaks. There was a trapdoor, right in the side of the sloping roof.

"Well, here goes," Dave said. He opened the trapdoor. Standing in the brilliant light and looking in, they could see nothing at all. Then they made out a square of light from the gable window. Kate held the trapdoor up and Dave leaned way in.

"I can't see anything . . ." he was saying.

Then a hand came from inside and grabbed his collar. He disappeared into the gray inside.

"Run, Kate, run," he cried.

Kate couldn't run and of course she wouldn't have anyway. She slid under the trapdoor and into the dark room. The trapdoor shut above her. Out of the golden light she could see a little, and then more and more. It was a tiny room, maybe six feet square, with a cot and a table and . . .

"Susan!" she gasped. "How did you get here?"

"Just the way you did," Sue said. "Did I scare you?"

"Scare me! If I'd had a weak heart, you would now be mourning over my lifeless corpse. You heard about the windows too."

"Yes, but look what I found," Susan said.

"You've got a real grip, Suze," Dave said. "I thought the ghost had me for sure."

"Oh, hush up about it now," Susan said. "Look what I found." She had a notebook, clothbound and thick. She leafed through the pages and they saw handwriting.

"This was the children's secret room," she said. "The book says so."

"What children?" Kate said.

"The children who lived here, stupid! Let's go downstairs and read it."

"Well, you may get excited about a book," Dave said, "but what I don't like is that cot. There's a sleeping bag on it. This must be where that fellow sleeps."

"Oh, nonsense," Susan said. "He couldn't get in

here from the ballroom and you're not going to make me believe he climbs around on the roof at night."

"Then where did that cot and sleeping bag come from?"

"They've probably been here all the time, just like all those funny things in the basement," Susan said. "You know perfectly well you imagined that man and you're just trying to bolster your story."

"Let's go down anyway," Kate said. "I don't like it here. Bring the book, Susan. We'll look at it downstairs."

They went back across the roof, again circled the chimney, descended the roof, crossed the flat roof, entered the little room, and then descended the back stairs.

"I'm going to tell Dad about that cot," Dave said.

"No, you're not," Susan said. "You'll spoil everything. At least let me read the book first. And it seems too bad to worry him anyway. Listen . . ."

From below came the sound of Dad's entrance. He was coming home, as usual, tired but game. They heard him say, "I'd like my sherry in the library."

"And then he'll go and pour himself a glass of sherry and sit in the library and read his paper," Susan said, "pretending he has a butler. He's as happy as a child. You just leave him alone. If this house is haunted or something is wrong, we'll find out for ourselves."

"Well, all right," Dave said. "It would be sort of mean to spring this on Dad."

"Susan," Mom's voice came from below, "come help me finish cooking dinner. Kate, will you set the table?"

"Oh, bother," Susan said. "I guess I better put this book away. And considering all the homework I've got, I guess we'd better wait until tomorrow."

"Give it to me," Kate said. "I can look at it after I do my homework."

"Nothing doing," Susan said. "This is my find, and if either of you say anything I'll never help you out again, no matter what trouble you get into. No matter if the ghost comes in your rooms."

"Don't worry," Kate said. "We won't say anything and anyway I'm too tired. Why didn't we stay in our nice little six-on-one ranch house?"

>»»»» **8** «««««

So THE EVENING PASSED, and the night, and it was the next day.

The fog pressed gray against the windows. The house was cold. Kate woke to a sense of impending doom and almost immediately a wave of homesickness swept over her. Why should I feel this now, she wondered, when I have so many other things to worry about and when I need all my courage for school? Why couldn't I have been homesick during the summer when I had nothing else to do? Another day of school, all those questions about her haunted house, those games in which she felt like an outsider, oh dear! Dave, staring from his bed at the fog, thought of the gorgeous football weather wasted, and of what good times his old friends were having. Then he thought with a sinking feeling of that bat-faced character lying somewhere above him, sleeping on his cot behind the hundredth window.

Susan, who didn't believe in the intruder, bat-faced or otherwise, wasn't worried about him, but she hadn't finished her lab report and her hair wouldn't go right. The curlers had slipped or something and one side went up and the other down. She brushed and brushed at it while Mom kept calling her to breakfast.

May was sitting up in bed, reading a library book and trying to feel a little pain somewhere. If she could be sick and have breakfast in bed and just stay here today, cozy behind the fog, how heavenly! But the pain wouldn't come, and she would have to get up. Oh, bother!

To Jody, burrowing bonily in his blankets, the idea of getting up was intolerable. He couldn't even open his eyes and he felt heavy as a stone, nailed to the bed. He'd been up late, writing a book on rockets. He couldn't get up, he couldn't, he couldn't.

But Mom made us all get up anyway, all except Dinky, who didn't have school. We all got down to breakfast and a sleepy, crabby crew we were.

"Well, look at the shiny morning faces," Dad said. He sounded pretty crabby himself.

"Sit up, Kate," he said, "and eat your oatmeal. Don't look so gloomy! What's the matter with you kids anyway?"

Kate wasn't eating because she couldn't swallow. She didn't want to talk either.

"She's homesick," Dave answered for her.

"Homesick!" Dad said. "Is that what's the matter with you kids?"

"I'm not homesick," Jody said. "I'm tired."

"Well, buck up, all of you," Dad said. "Have a little courage, a little backbone. Face the world with a smile! Bend it to your will!"

"Yes, sir," Dave said. He felt sorry for Dad, who obviously didn't want to go to work either.

"When I was your age I got up at four and walked miles on my paper route. Then home to breakfast and then another mile to school."

"You forgot the blizzards," Susan said.

"There were frequent blizzards," Dad said. "Susan, are you being impertinent? What's the matter with your hair?"

Susan got up with great dignity and left the room. Kate followed.

The fog was already lifting as we walked to school. Beams of fuzzy sunshine began to appear, and bits of sky. It cheered us. Jody began to run and the rest of us walked more briskly.

Well, school at last. Through the door, down the clattering hall, into the now familiar room. Today the kids looked more uniform, not so much like animals in the Ark, not so much rich and poor, or black, brown, white or yellow. Just a bunch of kids, Kate thought, all the same age, maybe not so different from her other school.

But there aren't so many just like me, not middle-class, white, Protestant. I'm a minority group too.

Well, so what? It's more interesting, isn't it, than just a bunch of kids, all alike? Like they say in the English stories, "It's a bit o' life, isn't it? I like a bit o' life."

Kate began to feel strong and calm and sensible. After all, she was smart enough. She'd read a lot of books and she'd always gotten good grades. She'd had lots of friends before and she would again. She was good at games. There was nothing to be afraid of. She looked around the room and thought everyone looked nicer today, even the teacher.

She stayed strong and calm and sensible for the first three periods. Her handwriting was slow and awkward, but it was a kind of challenge too, and as always arithmetic buoyed her up. Then, without warning and for no reason at all, the homesickness wave came back. It rose up in her throat like nausea and her eyes began to burn. In a minute she would be crying, right here in front of the whole class. She swallowed desperately and sent an agonized look at her teacher.

"What is it, Katherine?" Miss Brickle said. "Don't you feel well? Would you like to go out for a minute?"

Kate got up and almost ran out of the room. She went in the lavatory and shut herself in one of the

73

booths and cried. How silly, she kept saying to herself, how silly, just when you were getting along all right. Slowly the ghastly feeling in her throat subsided. She'd have to wash her face and wait a little until the crying didn't show quite so much, and then she could go back.

But, oh dear, there was someone else in the washroom. Someone running water, sniffing and yes, someone crying! What a vale of tears around here. Kate peeked out the door of her cubicle. It was Linda, and she must be hurt, Kate thought, because she was too mean to cry for any other reason.

"Are you hurt, Linda?" she asked. "Should I get the nurse?"

Linda glared at her. "No, I'm not hurt!" she snapped. She splashed cold water on her face. Kate just stood there. She knew Linda wanted her to leave, but it seemed odd just to walk out.

"You've been crying yourself," Linda said. "Are you hurt?"

"No," Kate said in a small voice. "I'm homesick."

"So am I," Linda said.

"You! How can you be homesick? You're at home, aren't you? You haven't moved or anything, have you?" Kate said.

"No, but I have to go to this school and I want to go back to my old school. We were all good friends there." Linda splashed more water.

"But why do you come here if you don't want to?"

Kate said. "I mean it must be a lot of trouble. You have to get a ride, don't you?"

"My daddy made me," Linda said. "He said now that they're giving us a chance to get out of the district and go to an integrated school, I've got to go. Integrated schools are better schools, he says."

Kate nodded. Everyone knew that.

"I tried to tell him I didn't want to come here, but he didn't pay any attention," Linda said. "He makes me so mad!"

"That's just the way Dad is," Kate said. "Either he doesn't pay any attention or he says, 'Buck up, be brave.' "

"My daddy said I should be glad to go to a better school and I can see my friends after school, but it isn't the same," Linda said.

"Is that why you're so mean all the time?" Kate asked.

"I guess I was pretty mean," Linda said. She grinned suddenly. "My daddy told me not to take anything from anybody and to stand up for my rights."

"Well, you certainly have been," Kate said.

"I just felt mean, that's all," Linda said. "But now I guess I'll just have to make the best of it."

"Me too," Kate said, "and anyway today is better than yesterday."

The door to the washroom opened and there was Miss Brickle.

"You girls!" she said. "I thought you were sick and you're just in here talking."

"We're better now, ma'am," Linda said meekly.

"I guess I'm not really sick," Kate said.

"Then come back to class," Miss Brickle said, but she didn't sound angry.

"Which just goes to show," Kate said to Dave as they walked home from school together, "that Negro fathers are just like white fathers, always making you do something for your own good. Anyway, I like Miss Brickle much better now."

"I had a pretty good day too," Dave said, "and I haven't seen that guy again, the one that hit me, I mean. I think he must go to some other school and was just hanging around that day. He might even go to junior high. He was pretty big."

"Maybe you'll never see him again," Kate said.

"Oh, I'll see him," Dave said. "I'm sure that's not the end."

They walked very slowly and reached home just as Susan's bus stopped at the door.

"Come on," she said, "I've been waiting all day. Let's go up and read that book."

"You mean you haven't read it yet?"

"No, I did all that homework and anyway some of it looked like code. I just decided to save it."

But when they went into the house, they found Mom in the living room with a visitor.

"Come in, children," she called. "Mr. Michelson, I'd like you to meet my children."

Mr. Michelson rose and came to them. He shook hands with each of them. Though he was scarcely taller than the children and rather gray all over ("a dear little gray man," Dinky called him), they saw now that he was not nearly as old as they had thought.

"Susan I know," he said, "and this is Katherine, and David. Delighted. Yes, indeed. And have you found any more treasure, my dear?" he said to Susan.

"She found my gingerbread man," Dinky said. Mr. Michelson looked down at Dinky and the gingerbread man.

"Why, dear me," he said, "that's Fred."

"Fred!" Mom said. "That's a much better name than 'gingerbread boy.' Shorter."

"Yes," Mr. Michelson said, "I know him well. He was owned originally by Virginia, who was the oldest, and passed down through the ranks. Paul had him at the end. Yes, yes. He was named for the family's handyman-gardener. The children had a great affection for him. He played a considerable part in family affairs."

"Which one do you mean, sir?" Dave asked. "Who played a part? This Fred or the other one?"

"Well, both, actually," Mr. Michelson said. "Both, but I was thinking of this one."

"Could you tell us something about the children?"

Susan asked. "We've found some things and we can't help being curious."

"Yes, do tell us," Mom said. "Has there been just the one family here?"

"Well, yes, yes, really just one family," Mr. Michelson said. "Other people have owned this house, but just one family really lived here. Until now, of course. Stanhope, their name was, as you probably know. There were six children and their parents, and the grandfather lived here as well. And then of course there were servants; it always took a lot of help to keep this place going. They had relatives living nearby and *they* had children and of course there were lots of friends, my family among them. What with the family and the relatives and the servants and other people dropping in, the house always seemed very full and so gay. Of course in those days there was a lot of money about." He looked around the room rather helplessly, as though trying to see where the money had gone.

"Yes, yes," he went on, "then in 1929 there was the crash, you know. Suddenly everything down the drain. Stanhope had very heavy losses, very heavy."

"How sad," Mom said.

"How romantic," Susan said. "I've always wanted to know someone who lost everything in the crash. Did he jump out a window?"

"Certainly not," Mr. Michelson said. "Quixotic he may have been, flamboyant, even eccentric, but he would never have taken his own life. No, he did a very silly, lovable thing. He called in all the servants, said he couldn't pay them and that he had lost everything and was moving back East. And with a great flourish he divided among them his then worthless stock."

"Worthless?" Mom said. "Was it really worthless?"

"Oh, everything was worthless then," Mr. Michelson said. "General Motors, if I remember correctly, stood at less than a dollar. Everyone thought it was just a sentimental gesture. Now, of course, things are different. I met Lizzy O'Leary just the other day. She used to be upstairs maid here. She's getting along in years now but she lives very comfortably on the stock Mr. Stanhope gave her."

"My goodness," Mom said, "what happened to the Stanhopes then?"

"Oh, they had a farm in New England. It had been in the family. They went back there. Mr. Stanhope went into a law firm with some members of his family or his wife's family, I forget which, and did very well. He died a wealthy man."

"So it all ended happily," Kate said. "Did they sell this house then?"

"Oh, no," Mr. Michelson said. "They always thought, you know, that they'd come back. An old aunt lived here with a housekeeper for years. She died during the war. The house was empty for some time. Then it was sold to a couple who hoped to make a rooming house out of it, but the neighborhood isn't zoned for that and the neighbors complained. There was an appeal that failed, I believe. Then it was rented for a while. Anyway, no one has really lived here, filling the house, that is, since the Stanhopes."

"Do you know, do you remember, where the Room of the Eyes is?" Susan asked.

"Oh my," Mr. Michelson said, "how that takes me back. That was a great institution, that was. Games started that way. Treasure hunts always began, *Go to the Room of the Eyes.* If one of the younger children misbehaved, Virginia — she was the oldest — would shut him up in the Room of the Eyes. There was a ritual connected with it too, with rhymes and sacrifices. Dear me, yes."

"But where is it?" Kate said.

"You don't know?" Mr. Michelson sounded astonished. "Why, it stands in the upstairs hall."

"How could a room stand in a hall?" Dave asked.

"But it wasn't a room, my dear boy. It was a wardrobe, a huge, black oak wardrobe. It was lined with an amazing wallpaper patterned in peacock feathers with golden eyes. You can't have missed it."

"I don't understand this conversation at all," Mom said, "but there's no wardrobe in the upstairs hall or anywhere else."

"It's not there?" Mr. Michelson asked. "Not there? Could it have been sold with the rest of the furniture?

Really, this is almost shocking! Where was Fred then? Fred always sat in the wardrobe."

"We found him in the ballroom," Susan said.

"Well, of course it was all a great many years ago," Mr. Michelson said. "Anything could have happened. It doesn't seem so long ago, but it was. Well, well, I must be going."

As Mom went to the door with him, Susan grabbed Dave and Kate.

"Come on," she said, "let's get up to the book before Mom starts asking questions."

"Gosh, yes," Dave said. He eyed the tea table in passing. "I'll bring the rest of the cake. It'll help us concentrate."

9

ＴHEY SAT on the rug before the fireplace in Susan's room and Susan began to read from the book.

"We, the children of E. G. Stanhope, being of sound mind and grown (most of us) too old for childish games, do give and bequeath to the children who come after us our toys, books, and games. We do not wish to leave our things to stupid children, but if you are smart enough to follow our clues your reward will be great. First direction, according to tradition (the last time of writing it) is:

> *Go to the Room of the Eyes.*
> *Hurry, faint heart ne'er won the prize!"*

"That's not much, is it," said Dave, "considering that they've hauled away the Room of the Eyes."

"Give me some cake too," Kate said. "Don't hog it all. What comes next?"

"Well, on the next page is a poem," Susan said. She read:

> *We leave our friend, dear Fred, behind —*
> *Fred is soft and wise and kind.*
> *In his wisdom keys he keeps,*
> *Guards the house and never sleeps.*
> *Fred unlocks the tops of boxes,*
> *Opens safes and winds up clockses.*
> *Guard well our friend, dear Fred, and he*
> *Will bring good luck to all of thee.*

"That's clear enough, isn't it?" Susan said.

"What does it mean about his unlocking boxes?" Dave asked. "Does that mean the handyman?"

"Search me," Susan said.

"What comes next?" Kate asked.

"It's kind of funny," Susan said. "It goes:

> *From Fred,*
> *To Fred,*
> *For Fred,*
> *In Fred,*
> *Go Fred,*
> *Find Fred.*
> *Fred, give Fred*
> *What is his.*"

"Now, that's just silly," Dave said. "Any more?"

"Yes," Susan said. "Then it says: *We also give,*

from our vast stores of experience, a comprehensive guide to this house and the neighborhood, but this is hidden from prying eyes by a code.

> *Pressed flower,*
> *Pressed book*
> *Will empower*
> *You to look.*

Then there's pages and pages of stuff in little tiny writing that must be their code. Could we solve it, do you think?"

"That last rhyme must be the clue, isn't it?" Kate said. "In stories the code is often taken from a book and that rhyme says *pressed book*. What does that remind me of?"

"Nothing that I can see," Dave said. "I hope it's almost dinnertime. I'm dying of hunger."

"You've just eaten half a cake," Susan said. "Well, when you press a flower you put it in a book and then you can put the book tight in a bookcase or put some other books on top of it. That would be a pressed flower in a pressed book."

"Or," Dave said, "you could put it in a vice and squash it."

"The book press!" Kate said. "There's a book press in the basement."

"You're kidding," Dave said. "I wouldn't know a book press if I saw one."

84

"It's just like one I saw in a magazine," Kate said. "It's a black thing with a big wheel on top."

"Let's go look," Susan said.

They ran down the back stairs and down the long hall, then down the basement stairs and into the big room.

"There it is," Kate said, "on that workbench." She crept around a dusty rocking chair, ducked under the old hat rack and took hold of the wheel on the press.

"Ugh, it's tight. I can't budge it."

"Let me try," Susan said.

"It probably needs some oil," Dave said. He watched in a tolerant, masculine way while his sisters struggled to raise the press.

"You try, Dave," Kate said.

"What are you doing?" a small voice asked.

"Who's that?" Susan asked. "Why, Dinky, where did you come from?"

Dinky's tiny figure emerged from behind a stack of rustic lawn furniture. She was very dirty and she'd been crying. The tears had washed clean streaks down her face.

"I've been here all the time," Dinky said.

"But what are you doing down here? What's the matter? You'll have to have a bath."

"I was hiding," Dinky said. She began to cry again; she rubbed her black hands over her eyes and then cast herself on Kate.

"Oh, Katie, that man tried to get my gingerbread man again," she said.

"Are you sure, Dinky? Are you making this up? She told us that the other day too," Kate said to Susan.

"He chased me and I ran down here," Dinky said.

"Where's Fred now?" Susan asked.

"In one of those chairs," Dinky said. "I wanted to put him in the cupboard, but I couldn't get the door open. There's too much stuff in front of it."

"What cupboard is that?" Susan asked.

"That great big one behind the furniture," Dinky said.

All looked where she pointed. There, rearing its black height behind the hodgepodge pile of bedsprings, wicker settee, picture frames and broken lamps, was an enormous black wardrobe.

"I never noticed it before," Susan gasped. "It can't have been here all the time. I've been down here a hundred times."

"Is it the Room of the Eyes?" Kate asked.

"Must be," Sue said.

"Jody and me found it," Dinky said. "It had a piece of cloth over it."

"Don't just stand there," Susan said. "Help me move this junk." They laid hands on the dusty mass and dragged it, piece by piece, out of the way. At last the great cupboard stood free; carved above, carved below, its smooth black finish shone dimly through the dust. Brass rings hung from brass lions' heads on each door. Susan grasped one and pulled. The door swung open. The wallpaper lining shone fresh and brilliant. The dim basement light showed the peacock blue feathers scattered on a white ground; it lit and brought to life the hundreds of golden eyes.

For a long moment they simply stared, awestruck by their discovery.

"Let's tell Mom!" Kate said.

"Gosh, yes," Dave said.

"No, don't tell her yet," Susan said angrily. "Wait till we find . . ."

But they were gone; their footsteps pounded on the stairs.

Susan got a chair and stood on it. She peered into the top compartment. Far back, stuck into a crack in the corner, was a yellowed piece of paper. She put it in her pocket. Then she went over to the press and with a great, grim pull turned the wheel and raised the press. A thin gray book lay between the halves of the press. She tucked it into the waistband of her skirt, under her uniform jacket.

"What are you doing now, Susan?" Dinky said.

"Never you mind!" Susan answered. "Do you want to leave Fred here, Dinky? I think he'd be safe upstairs now."

Mom came running down the stairs with Dave and Kate right behind her.

"What a mess!" she said. "We really must clean all

this out someday soon. So there it is, after all." She stared at the wardrobe, rubbed her hand over the satiny finish, and swung the doors open and shut.

"Well, I never," she said. "It's very handsome, isn't it? Will you look at those handles? We'll have that upstairs, though how we're going to move it I can't imagine. It'll be like moving the Cathedral. I don't see how they got it down here."

"I know what'll happen," Dave said. "Dad will say, 'Dave, move that upstairs,' and I'll just have to manage somehow."

Mom looked around at us. "My goodness, you're all filthy," she said. "All go upstairs and wash. Your father will be home any minute. Children, I'm just delighted. How did you happen to look down here anyway?"

"Oh, we were just poking around," Susan said vaguely.

"Well, come back upstairs now and get cleaned up for supper," Mom said.

As we topped the back stairs we heard the door slam and Jody calling Mom.

"Mom," he called, "come here. Someone has attacked Matthew!"

"Where are you?" Mom said. "Who's Matthew?"

Jody and a very disheveled-looking little boy were in the hall. The door opened again and Dad appeared.

"What's going on here?" he said. "Who was that

boy? Are you all right?" he said to the boy, who was apparently Matthew.

"I guess so," he said. There were dark red streaks on his face and neck and his shirt was torn.

"I never saw him before," Jody said. "He came right up on our lawn and grabbed Matthew and he said, 'You're Dave Evans's brother and I'm going to get you!' and he started to shake him. Then Dad came and he ran away up the street. Gosh! I guess he was really after me."

"An awfully big kid to pick on one this size," Dad said. "What do you know about this, Dave?"

"I don't know anything," Dave said.

"You better take Matthew home," Mom said to Dad, "and explain to his mother."

"Come on, Dinky," Susan said. "Let's go upstairs and wash." They started up. Dave and Kate followed.

"Come in my room," Susan said, "and tell me what's going on. I can see you and Kate both know."

"He's the guy who took those things from the Cathedral," Dave said. "At least we think so." He repeated the story of the first day of school.

"So that's where you got the black eye," Susan said. "Why don't you tell Dad? Or Mr. Michelson? Or the police? He's no friend of yours anyway."

"I can't do that," Dave said. "It would sound like I was trying to get him into trouble because he hit me."

"There isn't any evidence, is there?" Sue said.

"You know what, he must be in agony. He probably is a very superstitious type, you know. He wanted to do something very wicked so he stole something from the church. I don't suppose it was his own church. He wouldn't quite dare do that. He stole from another church instead and then when you told him about the rainbow it really scared him. He thinks the heavens are after him. If it weren't for you and Jody, I'd say serve him right."

"Do you think he'll try to steal Fred too?" Dinky asked fearfully.

"Heavens, no," Susan said. She picked Dinky up. "We're all just fine now. No one is hurt and you've got Fred and no one is going to steal him. Don't worry anymore, Dinky."

"Yeah," Dave said, "everything is great."

»»»»» 10 «««««

DINKY WOKE EARLY, for a change. It was Saturday, and the house was still. She lay looking around at her pink room and out the window at the misty gray sky. It was unusual for her to wake this early. She had, a short while before, had her fourth birthday and of course that meant she had learned to read. Susan had a rule that everyone had to learn to read before they were four. She was very strict, Susan was, and she ruthlessly dragged each of us through the first-grade readers. Dinky hadn't wanted to learn because she was afraid no one would read to her anymore, but Susan taught her anyway. Now that she could, at last, read almost everything, Dinky spent most of the day at it. She would hold Fred on her lap and read to him, looking frequently into his beautiful sympathetic face to be sure that he got the point of the story. She often read late at night, getting up to turn on her light when some disciplinarian had turned it out, and then sleeping late in the morning. She liked to come down the quiet stairs after the kids had gone to school and find Mom having a second breakfast while she read the mail. Actually, Mom was not much company to anyone these days. She went around muttering, "Peacock chairs, antique Kerman, toile d'Jouy," and eternally measuring windows.

Actually, although none of us noticed it until later, Dinky was growing thinner and paler. Her great blue eyes, surrounded by black lashes ("daisy eyes," Dave called them), had shadows under them. Her tiny hands were thinner. She was almost always lonely now, with the kids gone so much. She clung to dear, kind Fred and she worried terribly about him. Nobody seemed to believe her when she tried to tell about the man who wanted to steal Fred. She hated to go outside now. She was afraid of seeing him again.

Now, lying in bed under her pink quilt, she felt unreasonably sad. She clasped Fred to her and tried to think of something else. She had a little game she could play. She made her mind as blank as possible and then it would float away somewhere, somewhere where she was not Dinky Evans at all, but something immensely larger and different. How to explain it? For a long moment she would be something else, that's all, and she could never afterward describe how it felt, except that it was something very big. She had tried to tell Susan about this and Susan said, "Oh, Dinky, all little kids feel like that. You get over it when you get bigger." Now her mind swung clear somewhere, perhaps in the sky, like a constellation, and then came swirling back and she thought, But am I really Dinky Evans? Just one little girl named Dinky Evans? Is that all?

Dinky had been alone long enough. She had wondered, worried, dreamed, slept long enough. She jumped out of bed and ran to the door.

"Hi," Dad said, "are you the only one up? I can't see how you kids can be so lazy. I've just come back from a run." He was coming up the stairs, looking healthier than on weekdays, but also odder, in a gray sweat suit and tennis shoes.

"Let's get everyone up," he said, "and go down to the Market. It's a perfect day for it. The sun is coming out." Dinky looked out the landing window. Sure enough, great shafts of sunlight were breaking through the mist. The deep green of the laurel and holly gleamed sleek and wet, and even the chestnut, sadly casting its large yellowish leaves, looked momentarily cheerful.

"What's the matter, Dink?" Dad said, suddenly struck by her small paleness. "Off your feed? You're up too late, pounding the books. I've heard you."

"Can I take Fred to the Market?" Dinky asked.

"Fred? Who's Fred? The gingerbread boy? Sure,

he's probably been there before," Dad said. "Get some clothes on. I'm going to get everyone up."

"Good heavens," Dinky heard him saying to Mom, "how can you lie in bed on a beautiful morning like this?"

"I can lie in bed," Mom said angrily, "because I'm younger than you are. I haven't got middle-aged insomnia."

"If you'd come for a run with me," Dad said, "you'd feel better."

"If you went up and down stairs all day like I do," Mom said, "doing manual labor, you wouldn't need to run."

"What if I get the kids up and we'll go to the Market?" Dad said. "Dinky's up."

"Dinky! She must be sick!"

"She looks peaked," Dad said, and he strode off down the hall in his sweat suit to call the kids.

"Dinky, come in here," Mom said. "How do you happen to be up? Don't you feel well?" Dinky came in and leaned against Mom.

"I couldn't sleep," she said in a small voice.

"You look a little pale," Mom said, "and you're thinner. Come on, I'll fix you a nice breakfast. What would you like?"

"A pickle sandwich," Dinky said.

"Pickle, schmickel," Mom said. "Oatmeal and an egg. Come on, we'll have breakfast by ourselves. It's going to take a long time to get the kids up."

But Susan got up right away and came stamping downstairs flaming mad.

"Mom, why did you let Dad come pounding on my door like that? This is my Saturday morning and I'm going to sleep! I've worked late every night on that horrible homework and I'm going to sleep today. It's not fair to get me up like this!"

"Dad thought you'd like to go to the Market," Mom said mildly. "You're making an awful fuss over nothing, Susan, and I don't like to be shrieked at."

"I don't want to go to the Market," Susan said. "I don't want to go anywhere. I want to be left alone. Other people don't have to go on family outings at my age." She put two pieces of bread in the toaster and angrily shoved the handle down.

"You don't have to go," Mom said. "I thought you liked the Market."

"Not today," Susan said. She buttered her toast, put it on a napkin, and stalked out of the room.

"Well," Mom said, "I suppose all girls get temperamental when they get older, but I never thought my placid Susan . . . Oh well, she's probably just tired."

The rest of us were tired too, but breakfast put energy into us. By the time we were dressed and waiting in the sunny yard for Dad to finish shaving (first up, last ready, that's our dad), we were feeling fine.

Seattle is a long, narrow town, squashed between

96

Puget Sound and Lake Washington. To get to the Market, which is on the waterfront, you simply go downhill in a westerly direction. The car slid down óne sloping street after another, coming at last to the steepest ones of all, where the sidewalks have crosswise ridges to help you walk and a faulty parking brake is fatal. We parked on the side of a hill with the front wheels well wedged against the curb and climbed out of the car into a strange and wonderful world.

The wind blew fresh, the gulls wheeled and soared in the happy sky, the water was as blue as Dinky's eyes. Crowds of people, all sizes, ages, colors, costumes, converged here. The Market is a huge building, long and low, with many levels. Inside it always reminds us of an enormous cave, with a large, high, wide passage from which other passages branch. The main part has a broad aisle down the middle, full of people with market baskets, and on either side many, many small shops, or stalls, some hardly larger than stands. Here fresh vegetables are brought in and sold by truck gardeners; there are fruit stalls, meat markets, fish markets, spices, dried fruits. Nothing is packaged. Whole fish lie about in piles. Everything is in barrels, bins, or a state of nature. We saw vanilla beans for the first time, and peanut butter in huge crocks, cheeses as big as cart wheels, and great bloody hunks of meat with feet on them.

There is a lot of noise, because shopkeepers cry

their wares and the customers haggle. There are other things at the Market besides groceries. Down one sloping, ramp-like passage or another you find many little shops, hidden in the brick and plaster like caves in a cliff. There are jewelry shops and junk shops, antique shops and restaurants, shops which sell stained-glass windows and ship figureheads and totem poles, picture frames, Japanese screens, Chinese chairs.

If you look at magazines you get to thinking that people are all blond and handsome, with beautiful clothes and slim figures. In a real crowd of real people, like these at the Market, you see at once how silly this is. For one thing, there are many more dark people than light, and we don't mean just Negroes and Orientals either, and most people are too fat. No matter how beautiful clothes are in shops, they don't look the same on people, but look the worse for wear, like the people themselves. We like to see people who are buffeted by life, like ourselves. Evidently artists do too, because they are always at the Market, painting. But then, artists are perverse, and the Art Museum is full of pictures of things the urban renewal people are trying to get rid of.

Mom bought a bag of oranges from an old man who wore a white apron and had elastic bands on his shirtsleeves. He had a very kind pale wrinkled face and he patted Dinky on the head.

"What a wonderful age," he said. "All the world before you and not a care in the world."

"Little do you know," Dinky said, but she said it toward the floor and he didn't hear. She was getting tired of carrying Fred, but she hadn't dared leave him alone. When she looked down at his dear face, however, he looked so sympathetic that she turned him around so he could see the people.

Mom bought a box of apples which Dad took out to the car. She bought a salmon and gave it to Kate to carry. Dave had the oranges. She started pricing one-hundred-pound sacks of potatoes.

"I can't carry a hundred pounds of potatoes," May said. "I won't do it. I'll take Dinky and buy her a doughnut." She led Dinky off.

"Did she really think Mom would make her carry the potatoes?" Dave said.

"I would rather carry a hundred pounds of pota-toes than this smelly fish," Kate said. She moved back against a pillar and tried to see Dinky and May in the mass of people.

"Oh!" she said suddenly. "Why, some man just grabbed Fred away from Dinky!" As she said this, Dinky screamed. It was an awful scream.

"Fred! Fred!" she cried. She shot after the man who could be seen dodging toward the door. "He took Fred!" she shouted. Her voice rose high above the general babble and everyone turned to look.

A huge fat Negro woman with two bulging shopping bags stepped in front of the man.

"Give the little girl back her doll," she said. He dodged away from her and she hit him a swat with one of her shopping bags. He ran past the fruit stall where we'd bought the oranges.

"Stop, bring back that doll!" the man in the white apron shouted. He picked up an orange and threw it at the man.

The lady who had shown us the vanilla beans came out from behind her counter.

"Stop, stop!" she screamed. Across the aisle a man threw a tomato. It hit the thief on the back, but he flew on. He came to one of the halls and darted down it. Dinky was right behind. May followed her, then Jody. Kate and Dave dropped the oranges and salmon and ran too.

He ducked in an open door. We followed. It was a very small shop and we were moving fast. A wooden angel fell on its side. A medieval saint with candles in its hands rocked back and forth. A copper footbath fell with a clang as the thief leaped through another door and sped on. We ran through a restaurant and out the other door. Up the long hall we went, and now the slant was truly up. We were returning to the main floor, where the groceries were. The thief must not have known that, for when he suddenly came out into the open space, between a display of crab and a side of beef, he stopped dead.

There was a big, fine-looking man behind the butcher counter. He had rosy cheeks, a straw hat, and a white apron. He came out from behind the counter.

"Now, son," he said to our thief, "I don't know what your trouble is, but taking dolls from children is a strange way to behave. You just give me that whatever-it-is and then go home and sleep it off." He took Fred and gave him to Dinky. The man we'd been chasing walked right out the door.

"Well, what do you make of that?" Dave said.

"Say thank you to the nice man, Dinky," Kate said.

"Who was he? Why did he want Fred?" May asked.

Dad came hurrying up, and then Mom.

"What was all that fuss?" Mom asked.

"I kept your oranges and salmon," a lady said, coming up to us with our packages. We thanked everyone and everyone beamed at us. It was the nicest crowd we'd ever seen. As we passed out of the Market the shopkeepers all waved and the men in the meat market raised their hats. We felt like royalty as we walked through the smiling crowd, lugging our groceries.

When we got in the car Dinky was discovered to be shivering. Mom took her on her lap.

"What's the matter, Dinky?" she asked. "Did that man scare you?"

"He's always after Fred," Dinky said. "He's always hanging around."

"She keeps telling us someone is trying to take Fred," Kate said. "We didn't believe her, but I guess someone really is."

"Why wasn't I told about this?" Mom asked. "What would anyone want with Fred?"

"Probably crazy," May said.

"Raving mad," Jody said. "There are lots of crazy people up in the park."

"That's enough," Dad said. "No use scaring ourselves."

When we got home, Mom took Fred and locked him in the pantry so Dinky could stop worrying. Dave and Kate went up to tell Susan. Each privately thought that the man who had kidnapped Fred must also be the man who came up to the third floor that night. But who wanted to think of a thing like that?

"Susan, Susan," they called, "where are you?"

"We've got something to tell you," Dave bellowed.

"Up here," came Susan's voice, very far away.

She was in one of the closets under the eaves. They went through the old ballroom and found her.

"What are you doing in there?"

"Hunting for clues," she said. "I've found something, though. Look here."

The closet was long and narrow, with one straight

wall and one steeply slanted wall that was the ceiling as well. At the back of this long triangle Susan was standing with a flashlight.

"There's a door here, see? It just looks like part of the wall. There's another closet behind this one and that's the room where we found the book." She pulled the door open and there, sure enough, were the dusty window, the table and chairs, the cot and sleeping bag that belonged to the secret room.

"So that's where he went that night he walked through your room when you were asleep," Susan said.

"You said we imagined it," Dave said.

"I guess I was wrong," Susan said.

"Then why on earth didn't he take Fred then?" Kate said. "Fred was right there! He was just lying on the floor out there. The man could have taken Fred then and not come around now frightening Dinky."

"You don't believe what Dinky said, do you?" Susan said.

"That's what we came up here to tell you. There was a man at the Market, it must have been the same one. He took Fred and ran and we all chased him and people threw things at him and he knocked over an angel and ran through a restaurant and then a man in the meat market got Fred back."

"My goodness," Susan said, "what did Mom say?"

"She was buying potatoes and Dad was taking the apples out to the car. Dinky was sort of sick and Dad said not to frighten her anymore."

"My goodness," Susan said again, "what did he look like?"

"Nothing much," Kate said, "young and ordinary."

"Young?"

"I thought he would be old and horrible, with a face like a bat's," Dave said, "but he looked like anyone else."

"Maybe we should tell Dad that he sleeps up here," Susan said. "How did he happen to go to the Market anyway?"

"I suppose he listens," Kate said. "He creeps around and watches us and listens. Isn't it awful?"

They thought about the general awfulness for a while and then Susan said, "But it's interesting, anyway. It takes my mind off my troubles."

"You don't have any troubles," Dave said. "You don't have anyone waiting around to beat you up or anything."

"No, but I have Mom and school and all these lab reports," Susan said.

"What were you doing up here anyway?" Kate asked.

"Didn't I tell you? Doing the treasure-hunt clues. I was doing fine until I got this far. Look, I'll show you." They went out into the ballroom and sat on the window seat.

"Now, this is the first clue," she said, "the one I found in the Room of the Eyes." She handed Kate a yellowish folded-up piece of paper. Kate read out:

Wring, wring, what shall I wring?
The cat's run away with the pudding-bar string.
Wring it dry, read and try
To see it for yourselves.

"That one's pretty easy," Susan said, "with all those *wring's* in it."

"You mean," Kate said, "that it's that old washing machine with the hand wringer on it?"

"Yup. Stuck in the wringer."

"They took an awful chance," Dave said. "How could they think no one would even turn that wringer for almost forty years? Or that it would even be there?"

"Well, it is here and no one did turn it," Susan said, "and what I think is, well, Mr. Michelson said they always expected to come back. I think this was just for the fun of it. Anyway, it must have been the younger ones who planned it. If the house was built in 1910, and if all the children were born here, then in 1929 the older ones would be almost grown up. Probably the younger ones were ten or eleven and they didn't think things out much."

"What was in the wringer?" Kate asked.

"A picture, a photograph. Here."

The print was in a half-moon. It was small, dark, and cracked.

"I can't see anything," Kate said, squinting at it.

"Let me see," Dave said.

"It looks familiar," he said, turning it up the other way, "but I can't tell what it is. Is it wood?"

"It took me a long time, but I got it," Susan said. "Should I tell you?"

"I guess you better."

"It's a close-up of the design on the library mantel. And the next clue was stuck in between the mantel and the wall. I got it out with a nail file."

"Funny someone dusting didn't take it out years ago," Dave said.

"That mantel is so high you have to stand on a chair to see," Susan said.

"What did that one say?" Kate asked.

Susan unfolded the paper and read:

Partway up and partway down,
Try it in between.
Five stairs down or five stairs up,
The mystery is seen.
Here it's always winter,
Here it's never spring,
Here begins the Yuletide,
Here Christmas joys begin!

"But there's nothing partway up the stairs," Dave said, "certainly nothing to do with Christmas. Do they mean the landing? Did they have a Christmas tree on the landing?"

"Perhaps the children all crept down the stairs and looked over the banister, watching for Santa Claus," Kate said in a dreamy voice. "I can just see them, all in white nightgowns and maybe nightcaps, like in 'A Visit from St. Nicholas.' "

"It wasn't all that long ago," Susan said.

"It's a long time," Kate said. "They must all be grandparents with gray hair and maybe false teeth. Just look at Mr. Michelson."

"Anyway," Susan said, "you're way off. It's the other stairs."

"The back stairs?" Kate said.

"There's a cupboard halfway up the back stairs," Dave said. "Oh, I get it. They kept the Christmas ornaments there."

"Right!" Susan said. "There's still some tinsel there."

"The clue was lying on the floor, I suppose?" Dave said. "Because personally I think you're making this up as you go along."

"No, stupid, it was stuck on the inside of the doorframe. And if you think I can write like that or make pages look this yellow . . ."

"All right, all right, what does it say?"

"It says:

Under the eaves,
Buried in leaves.

That's why I came up here, but I've been through all these places under the eaves and there aren't any leaves at all."

"Slipped up at last," Dave said. "Probably put leaves there and somebody swept them up."

"Let's look again anyway," Susan said.

They went back in the closet, switched on the flashlight, and looked around. Since there was nothing there but a stack of boards on the floor, it didn't take long to look.

"Those are pretty boards," Kate said. "We could make something out of them."

"They're not boards," Dave said. "They're table leaves. See the holes and pegs."

"Table leaves!" Kate said. "Who's dumb now? *Buried in leaves.*"

Sure enough, when the leaves were moved, there was a piece of paper on the floor. Dave snatched it up.

Last one was a pun,
Lowest form of humor.
For this one you will have
To do more.
Climb the prickly holly,
Or mount the cherry tree.

Turn left at the bole,
And find the hole.
Ask Fred to bring the key.

"I suppose," he said, "that that does mean the cherry tree at the side of the house? That great big one?"

"It's an awfully old tree," Susan said, "but it must have changed a lot in all this time."

"If we should find it, it wouldn't help," Kate said, "because it says, *Ask Fred to bring the key.* That must be the handyman and he isn't here anymore."

"It's crazy," Susan said, "but let's look anyway."

They stopped in Susan's bedroom to leave the clues and then trooped down the back stairs, dusty, disheveled, and elated.

The cherry tree was formidable and beautiful, as tall as the house. Its thick black trunk was twisted at the base but then sprang straight up and spread its gracious branches high above them.

"We'll have to get a ladder to get started," Dave said. "I can't get up to any of those branches."

"If you'll give me a boost up to that bump up there," Kate said, "I think I can do it. But it's so big. Where do we look?"

"*Turn left at the bole,*" Susan said. "That's that big bump, isn't it?"

"I think bole just means the trunk," Dave said. "I'll boost you up, Kate. There's no use climbing way up. This was a smaller tree when that rhyme was written. Look for a hollow or a fork where they could stick a box."

"Why a box?"

"Well, it's supposed to have a key, isn't it?"

"Who is that old lady coming up the walk?" Susan whispered. "I think she's coming here."

Along the walk came an elderly woman, thin as a twig and walking briskly. She looked up at the house and the children with a bright, friendly stare and put her head on one side like a bird. She was a little like a sandpiper.

"Hi," she said, "hiding something? Do you mind if I sit here on the bank and have my lunch? I often came along here and sat when the house was empty, and thought about old times."

She sat on the grass and opened the paper bag she was carrying. She took out a napkin, spread it on the grass beside her, and laid out lettuce, celery, a carrot, and a cut-up tomato.

"My niece says I eat like a bird," she said, "but what I say is, eat the way I do and you'll feel good when you're past seventy. I'm going to live to a hundred, I am." She took a bite of celery.

"Don't let me stop you," she said. "If you're up to something, go ahead. I never stopped the Stanhope kids unless they got in my way. 'Keep out from under my feet,' I'd say, 'and I won't say a word about your tricks.'

"Why," she said, "I just thought. You don't know who I am, do you? I'm Lizzy O'Leary. I used to work here, many years ago. My, I'm glad to see children here again. Lonesome, the house looked. No curtains, no flowers, no wash on the line. 'Twill be different now, eh? Fun and games, eh?"

"Were you here when the Stanhope children were little?" Susan asked. She came away from the cherry tree and sat down by Lizzy O'Leary. Kate and Dave followed.

"Are you the one Mr. Stanhope gave the stock to?" Dave asked.

"I am that," she said. "I came to work here when I was sixteen. Ah, the dear man, what a one he was! And I not thinking a thing of it until the dividend checks began to come in! 'I'm cheating you out of your salary, Lizzy,' he said, 'for 'tis flat broke I am, but I'll give you what I have, though it's worth little enough.' "

"We found this treasure-hunt clue," Sue said. "Can you tell who wrote it?" Lizzy took the paper and held it at arm's length.

"My eyes are as good as ever," she said, "but my arms are a mite short. Yes, that will be Paul, the silly little tyke. He was always hiding things. *Ask Fred to bring the key*, eh? Well, Fred's been gone a long time. He's probably dead. He was a good deal older than I. He went back to Alaska."

"Do you think it's this cherry tree?" Susan asked.

"Must be," Lizzy said. "There was a holly tree right next to it, but that was cut down years ago. Climb up and see. Ah, to think, after all these years . . ."

Dave gave Kate a boost and she pulled her thin length up the trunk to the lowest branch. She looked down at them, at the gray-haired old lady, as eager as a girl, and at Susan and Dave, expectant.

"What do I do now?" she asked.

"Just look around," Dave said.

She peered here and there, climbing higher.

"There's a hollow here," she said, "full of leaves. There's some chestnuts too. The squirrels must use it. Ugh, bugs. Here's a box, a tin box. Wait a sec. Here it is." She pulled it out and held it for them to see.

"Here, I'll drop it." She dropped it into Dave's outstretched hands and then swung from the branch and dropped down herself.

"It's locked, sure enough." Dave held out the small metal box.

"Pretty rusty," Susan said. "Look, those little screws will pull right out. We don't need Fred's key after all."

"I remember that box," Lizzy said. "He was always carrying it around."

The rusty screws pulled out of the rusty lock and the lock fell out in Susan's hand. Dave opened the box and Kate snatched the note inside.

Spare the rod and spoil the child
Find the rod, your wish fulfilled
  (George wrote this. He isn't good at rhymes).

"And there's a drawing," Kate said, "like a spear-head."

"I know what that is," Lizzy said. "It's the end of the wooden curtain rod in the cook's old room. I'll show you if you like."

"Yes, come in, Lizzy," Susan said. "Mom would like to meet you."

"There used to be hanging flowerpots here," Lizzy said as they crossed the porch.

"Mom," Susan called, "here's Lizzy O'Leary, who used to work here. We're going upstairs."

"I'll be right there," Mom called back.

"Come upstairs first," Kate said.

"Cook had the front room," Lizzy said as she led the way up the back stairs. "It was bigger than mine, but not as pretty."

"My word," she said as they entered the front third-floor bedroom. "This wallpaper is new since my day. Pretty awful, isn't it? Makes the whole room look different."

"The last people who owned this house, the ones who were going to make a rooming house out of it, did a lot of rooms over," Susan said. "Mom says as awful as this is, it will be a long time before we get around to changing it."

"Seems different in here, somehow," Lizzy said, "but then I never was in here much. Cookie and I didn't get along. Now here's the curtain rod and the end unscrews to get the rings on and off."

The window was low beneath the slanted ceiling. Dave lifted the rod down and unscrewed the end. Rolled up inside was the expected bit of paper. He read:

Hot grow I, very hot,
Yet I can't burn.
Safe in the brick am I,
Safe in the stone. . . .

"Susan, Kate," Mom called from below, "come down. Bring Lizzy down."

"We'd better go down and finish this later," Sue said.

"There's more to the clue," Dave said.

"It'll keep, I guess," Susan said. "Give it to me and we'll come back later."

They started back downstairs. Lizzy began to laugh.

"I feel just like Fred," she said, "that old coot. He'd play any game. Loved those kids, he did. I'd tell him, 'If you'd spend half as much time on your work as you do playing, this place would be ship-shape.' But that didn't matter. He loved the kids and they loved him, I guess. In fact, George and Paul seemed to think he was just their age. Treated him like a great friend, they did. He'd have liked this, he would."

>>>>>> **II** <<<<<<

SUNDAY MORNING, and Dave was waking up and, moreover, waking up happy. Before he even opened his eyes, or stretched, he felt happy, as though he'd had a good dream. About time too. For months, it seemed, he'd awakened sad, worried, apprehensive, or homesick. He knew well enough what made the difference. In the last few days he had gotten acquainted with a new gang of boys, and at last it was beginning to look as though he was going to be part of a group again. Man, how lonely he'd been! Lonely enough, he now realized, to have joined any sort of gang. In search of companionship he'd have even joined one of those city gangs you read about, with switchblades and broken bottles. Well, luckily for him, these new friends were nice guys — almost, by his old standards, too nice. They all had paper routes, for instance, and paid their school fees and bought their own clothes out of the money they made. They all went to the same school and church; their lives revolved loyally around church, family and each other. They went to parochial school, that's why he hadn't met them before. For the sake of such an organized, friendly life, how gladly would he become a Catholic too!

The morning was chilly, but the high, colorless sky was cloudless. Another good day, with football in the afternoon. He threw on some clothes and ran downstairs. Mom was sitting at the kitchen table, drinking coffee and reading the Sunday paper.

"Hey, Mom," he said, "can I go to Catholic school next year?"

"No," she said.

"Why not?" he said. "What's wrong with that? Do you think they'd convert me or something?"

"No," Mom said, "you can't go to Catholic school because you're not a Catholic. They've got enough to do educating their own. You've got your own school."

"I should think I could go to school with my own friends," Dave persisted.

"It's just about time," Mom said coldly, "that you grew up a little. It's time you got over the idea that you have to be part of a close group. You've got to stand on your own feet. Your father and I want you to know all kinds of people and have friends in all groups."

"But, golly, Mom, everyone belongs to some group, and it's so much easier."

"I know that," Mom said grimly. "Now start your breakfast. I'm going to get Dad and the kids up and maybe we'll take a picnic and go to the zoo. This is probably the last nice Sunday."

"To the zoo!" Dave said. "You mean a family outing to the zoo like the Bobbsey twins? I'm going to play football with the guys."

Mom ignored him and stalked out of the kitchen. But she was angry, at him or the world, and as she went on upstairs she got angrier.

There was a sign on Jody's door saying "Keep out," and one on Dinky's door saying "Come in." Mom snatched them both off and frowned at the holes the tacks had made. Then she opened Jody's door. She looked across the sea of trains, blocks, books, maps, papers, crayons, and bits of airplanes to Jody's bed.

"Get up, Jody," she said. "How do you get your room in this shape? This is terrible!"

Jody opened one eye, as blue as a harebell, and stretched his bones and sinews.

"Gosh, Mom, I don't know," he said. "Sometimes when I wake up at night I hear strange sounds and I think it's those darned toys falling from their places."

"Get up and pick them up right away," Mom said. Then she went into Dinky's room.

"Get up, Dinky," she said. "It's the middle of the morning. Get dressed and put on your shoes. No more coming down barefoot. And get Kate to braid your hair."

"But I always eat breakfast in my bathrobe!" Dinky cried.

"Not today," Mom said. Then she went along the hall and woke up May, Kate, and Susan. To Susan she said, "Come downstairs right away, Susan. I want to talk to you."

Dinky flew down the hall to Kate's room.

"Oh, Katie, Katie," she wailed, "Mama's after me."

"She's after all of us," Kate said. "We'll just do what she says and she'll forget it pretty soon."

Susan had spent a quiet hour sitting up in bed working on the code part of the Stanhope book. She hadn't gotten it yet, but she was hot on the trail. She felt like the man who deciphered Samuel Pepys' diary. When Mom came pounding on the door she interrupted an intricate train of thought. By the time Susan got downstairs she was as angry as Mom.

"You wanted to talk to me?" she said icily.

"Yes," Mom said, "and sit down. Don't stand there looking like a minuteman. I stopped by your school yesterday and Miss Massingham tells me you're doing *C* work in mathematics."

There was a bellow of rage and pain from the doorway. "A *C* in math!" Dad shouted. "Susan!"

"She also said," Mom went on, "that you never do C work. Your work is either brilliant or flunking, she said. In fact, some days you don't do any work at all. In other words, it's pure laziness. When I think how hard your father works to send you there!"

"Oh, Mom," Susan said. "I didn't ask to go to private school. It was your idea. I go at eight in the morning and get home at four, and then I'm supposed to do four hours of homework. Grownups don't work twelve hours a day. Why should I? I got the highest grade in my whole class in the achievement test. What difference does it make whether I do my daily work?"

"But it goes on your college record."

"I don't care about my college record!" With these profane words Susan rose and left the room.

"I guess I'd better make another pot of coffee," Mom said.

"I don't see," May said in a high, complaining voice, "why you make such a fuss about Susan's grades. You never pay any attention to my grades. I could practically flunk out of school and you wouldn't care. You don't care about me at all."

"Why, May," Mom said, "of course I care about you. But you're just a little girl. You get very good grades anyway. I don't want to push you at your age."

"When Muriel got a *B* last year her mother wouldn't let her watch TV for a month and her big brother wouldn't even speak to her. They care what grades she gets!"

"Who is Muriel?" Dave asked. "Is she that Chinese girl with glasses? Does she get all *A*'s?"

"But Muriel's mother was born in China," Mom said. "I was talking to her at the last PTA meeting. All immigrants feel strongly about education."

"Immigrants! How can you call my friends immigrants!" May said furiously.

"What's wrong with that?" Mom said. "That's what they are. I'm not maligning them." But May was stamping angrily out of the room.

"I'm spending the day at Muriel's," she said. "We're working on our social studies notebooks, so don't count on me for anything."

"That's all right, May," Dave said. "Life is tough. Grin and bear it."

"Huh!" May said. "You grin and we've all got to bear it!"

"Listen here, tin teeth!" Dave began.

"All right, all right," Dad said tiredly. "Come back and sit down. The day is sort of falling to pieces, isn't it? Maybe your mother and I had better go someplace by ourselves and leave you kids to cope with your spleen."

"That's a good idea," Mom said. "But what's gotten into Susan anyway?"

"She's probably found out she doesn't have enough money to belong to the real 'in' group at her school

123

and she isn't poor enough to be a scholarship type. She's tired of not belonging to a group, just like me," Dave said.

"Groups!" Mom said. "Crowds, groups, gangs! I'm sick of them. May wants to be Chinese, you want to be Catholic, Susan wants to belong to heaven knows what. If that's what's worrying her, why doesn't she say so?"

"Because we look kind of silly complaining," Dave said. "After all, you and Dad do the best you can, don't you? And with the war on poverty and share-croppers and slums and everything, how can kids like us complain?"

"Quite right," Dad said, "so don't do it. I'm going to get dressed and then I'm going for a long walk."

Actually, Dad and Mom went someplace in the car, first giving long instructions as to the cleaning of Jody's room, the creation of dinner, the care of Dinky, etc. Dave escaped to his football game, and May went over to Muriel's.

May came home about four o'clock. The day, which had been fine, was drawing in. It was growing dark and cold and the fog was mizzling in. The house was warm and bright and smelled deliciously of roasting lamb. May went into the kitchen to get something to eat. Jody and Dinky were there. They had found all the water pistols in the house, quite a lot, and were filling them with sudsy ammonia and vinegar.

"What on earth are you doing?" May asked. "That ammonia is poison."

"We're not going to drink it," Jody said. "We're going after a criminal. Kidnappers don't deserve any mercy."

"Oh, just a game," May said. "Well, don't shoot at each other and don't shoot in the house."

"Fred is in the hands of the enemy," Dinky said, putting a water pistol in each pocket and two in her belt. "We're going up in the park after him."

May wasn't listening. She was remembering that she had a Butterfinger in her room and that there were peanuts and bananas left from last night's curry.

"Don't be late for supper," she said. When they were gone she gathered her loot and went upstairs to lie on her bed and read and eat.

Presently Susan came in. "Where's Dinky?" she asked. "I can't find her."

"Out playing with Jody," May said, concealing the rest of the peanuts.

"Well, I hope she put her jacket on," Susan said. "It looks awfully gray and cold out."

Time passed, and presently Dave returned. "Hi, where is everyone?" he called.

"Up here," Kate shouted back.

"Mom and Dad home yet?"

"No."

"Getting pretty dark," he said. "Boy, am I hungry."

Susan and Kate came downstairs.

"Have you seen Dinky and Jody?" Susan asked. "They're out playing somewhere."

"No, but they better come in," Dave said. "Let's lay a fire. Dad'll appreciate it." He and Kate went to get logs while Susan went to look for the children.

"I can't find them anywhere," she said, coming in. "Go up and ask May where they went, Katie."

Kate went up and talked to May.

"She said it was some kind of a game," Kate said. "They said Fred was in the hands of the enemy and they were going up in the park after him."

"But they're not allowed in the park, at least Dinky isn't," Susan said, "and it's getting dark. What's the matter with May anyway?"

"I think she thought it was just pretending," Kate said. "She said they took water pistols full of ammonia."

"Come on," Dave said, "we better find them before Mom and Dad get home."

"Here are Mom and Dad," Susan said. "We'll have to tell them."

Mom and Dad came in, looking young and cheerful.

"What a gorgeous day," Dad said. "We drove up to Mt. Rainier. Beautiful. Fire, eh? Good for you. Getting cold. Boy, am I hungry!"

"Is something the matter?" Mom asked. "You children look worried. Where's Dinky?"

"Well, that's just it," Susan said. "She and Jody went out somewhere. May says they went up in the park after Fred."

"After Fred?" Dad said. "What's going on here, anyway? Why all this fuss about Fred?"

"May says?" Mom repeated. "Why did May let them go? Where were you, Susan? You were baby-sitting."

"I was upstairs," Susan said miserably, "and May thought they were just pretending."

"Well, come on," Dad said. "I'll take Dave and Kate. The rest of you stay here. They may come home anytime. Get some coats, kids, it's cold. Better have some flashlights."

"Listen, Dad," Dave said, "that park is no place to be after dark."

"Of course it isn't," Dad said. "That's why we're going after them. They may be lost."

"I don't mean that, Dad," Dave said. "I mean it's dangerous. I mean I think you should call the police. We were up there the other night, these guys and I, and we met a policeman. A plainclothes policeman. He showed us his papers. He said not to come up there after dark because it was no place for kids."

"Ridiculous!" Dad said. "Nonsense! What do you think this is, Central Park? I won't call the police just to look for my own kids in a park right behind my house. Besides, I'm a taxpayer. If I want to take a picnic up there, I will."

"But the man who took Fred may be crazy," Kate said. "Look how he ran through the Market."

"At least take a club or something," Dave said.

"I'll tell you what," Dad said. "That *was* a funny deal at the Market. Let's take the swords. They won't cut butter, but they frighten people."

We had three swords. One was Japanese and two were German parade swords. Dad got them and gave one to Kate and one to Dave.

"I'll take my blank gun too," he said.

"Jody and Dinky have water pistols full of ammonia," Susan said.

"Good grief," Dad said, "we'd better hurry. Anything may have happened. Don't worry," he said to Mom. "Back soon."

"Don't worry," Mom said. "Don't worry! Why do people say things like that? Come on, Susan, let's peel potatoes. There's always work."

Out into the darkness went Dad, Kate and Dave. They crossed the strip and the road, and entered the park woods. Shadows enveloped them. The trunks of trees stood just a little blacker than the air between the trees. Their footsteps were loud in the dry leaves. Their swords banged awkwardly against their legs.

"Should we shout?" Dave asked.

"Wait till we get up to the clearing," Dad said. "Then we'll blink the light and yell."

"No telling who's lurking around here," Dave said.

128

"Am I raising a coward?" Dad said. "You're afraid of everything lately."

They passed through the wood and came to a great open space, woolly with white shadows, arched over by a thick and lightless sky.

"Fog," Dad said in a despairing voice. It moved here and there, the fog did, now pressing close up to us and now receding. Trees, patches of grass, bits of each other, all were visible for moments and then swallowed up, gone. Our voices echoed queerly. No one answered our shouts. We saw no one. And yet, somehow, we didn't feel alone.

There were lots of people in that park. We knew it. We couldn't see them or hear them. Likely they couldn't see us. But we could tell they were there. Who would they be? Derelicts? Tramps from Skid Road? Gangs of kids? Thieves? Ghosts? Jody and Dinky? Who?

For a long time we tramped around, our footsteps now loud, now muffled, our voices echoing futilely. Now we walked isolated in a room that moved with us, now the fog blinded us completely. Uphill, downhill, sideways. Dad strode on ahead of us.

"He's so brave," Dave said sullenly. "How long is it since someone punched him in the stomach, I wonder?"

"He leads a sheltered life," Kate said.

We came to the top of the hill. The air was clearer here, and the streetlights shone fuzzily through it.

We passed the museum and then the conservatory. We started down the other side of the hill.

"Let's stop and rest a little," Dad said.

He led the way to a picnic table and we sat down on the benches. The streetlight shone directly overhead and we sat there as on a lighted stage, surrounded by fog and darkness. The light funneling down on us gave an illusion of warmth. It was oddly peaceful.

Dad ran his hands through his hair, where the drops of moisture showed on his crew cut.

"I'm wet as a rat," he said. "What should we do now? We're not getting anyplace. It must be seven o'clock."

"Look there," Kate said.

Coming soundless through the fog, swimming, it seemed, was a large white figure. It came out of the fog and into the circle of light and we saw that it was a great big woman in a nurse's uniform. A cape hung far back on her shoulders. She strode heftily to the table.

"Excuse me," she said in a harsh treble, "but I couldn't resist coming to see what you were doing. You look so domestic. Are you having a picnic?" Her large eyes looked us over. She must have seen our swords.

"Actually, we're looking for two small children," Dad said. "They went out to play a game about three hours ago. We've been looking for some time." He ran his hands over his wet hair and face again. He looked exhausted.

"What a night to be lost in!" the nurse said. She looked around at the fog and shivered. "Don't you think you should call the police?"

"Yes," Dad said, "in a minute we'll go home and do that. You shouldn't be here yourself, should you? Aren't nurses warned not to walk in lonely places after dark?"

"You're right," the nurse said. "It was foolhardy, but I thought a short cut . . ." But she didn't seem in much of a hurry after all, because she came and sat on the bench beside Dad.

We all sat there without saying anything for a while. How silly, we thought. Why are we sitting here, with Jody and Dinky lost somewhere and a crazy man loose in our lives?

Then we realized that Dad and the nurse were listening, and we began to listen ourselves. All around us, in the darkness, there was a little rustling, a little pattering, as though tiny animals were closing in on us. We strained our ears. We waited.

Into the ring of light, yelling, sprang many small figures. Grinning faces popped up around us. Arms were raised, broken bottles caught the light.

Kate and Dave dove under the table. Dad and the nurse, with surprising agility, disentangled themselves from the picnic benches and faced the throng, back to back.

"Kids!" Dad said disgustedly. "Little kids! You can't hit them."

"I can!" the nurse shouted in a joyous bellow. She grabbed the nearest two and banged their heads together. She picked up two more and threw them away. She grabbed another one and, turning him over her massive knee, gave him several sharp swats.

"Aha!" Dad shouted. "Good for you, nursie!" He kicked viciously right and left to give himself room and drew his Japanese sword.

"American soldier, you die!" he shouted.

Dave and Kate scrambled up from under the table, brandishing their swords.

"God for Harry, England, and St. George!" Dave shouted.

"Come on, men," Kate bellowed, "close in! Off with their heads!" The swords flashed grimly in the streetlight.

In a minute it was all over. The kids had scattered. We sheathed our swords and looked at the damage. Nurse had some cuts on her hands and Dad had a gash on his cheek. They looked at each other and grinned.

"You're a very active nurse," Dad said.

"Those kids," Nurse said, "give me the willies, and I don't willy easy. Should we go on with our picnic?" We sat down again in our pool of light. The fog was thinning a little, and we could see the empty wading pool, like a crater on the moon.

Dad reached in his pocket and took out his pipe and tobacco. Then he took out his blank gun and laid it on the table.

"Blank gun," he said to Nurse, and began to fill his pipe.

This time we hadn't long to wait. A figure in a long raincoat came swaggering up to the table. There were other, darker figures in the shadows. This one had a puffy, bad-tempered face with big jowls and a small useless-looking nose.

"What do you think you're doing here?" he said, only he used a great many more words, both unnecessary and rude.

Dad lit his pipe very slowly, blew smoke in the mean-looking face, and said, "We're having a picnic."

"What's it to you?" Nurse said in a high, mincing voice.

The man said in a very nasty way that we'd better leave, it was his park, and did they want any harm to come to the kids? Dad said he'd sit there as long as he pleased and Nurse said she would too. Then all the creeping shadows gathered themselves up and piled on Dad and Nursie.

Dave jumped up on the table and grabbed the blank gun, which he fired twice. Kate, realizing that her sword would do no good, took off the scabbard and banged at the fellows attacking Dad. Someone blew a whistle. The fog of battle obscured the action, but a number of bodies seemed to be flying around. There was a siren, a squeal of brakes, and two policemen trotted into the mess.

"Is that you, George?" they said.

"Sure is," Nurse said cheerfully. Then the guns came out, and the handcuffs. They led several dark figures off and one they carried. We were alone again under the streetlight.

"Where did you learn karate?" Nurse asked Dad.

"In the Commandos," Dad said.

"I was at Anzio myself," Nurse said, and they shook hands.

Nurse sat down on the bench and put her ham-like arms on the table. There were tattoos on her arms.

"Oh, you're a policeman," Dave said.

"True for you, son," Nurse said, "and I want to thank you all for helping us out tonight. We didn't get the kids, of course, but we weren't after them. This other gang we've been trying to decoy out for some time. They're small-time, you know, but they do a lot of harm and they're potentially dangerous. Too bad they hang around here, but there it is, they do."

Dad sat down too. "You were right, Dave," he said. "This park is no place for kids."

"Gosh, Dad," Dave said, "I always thought of you

as more of a brain worker. You did real well in that fight."

"It's just a knack," Dad said. "It comes back."

"It hasn't done you much good, though, has it?" the policeman said. "Your kids are still missing."

"You're right!" Dad said. "I forgot them for a minute. Nothing like a fight to make you forget your troubles."

"I hear something," Kate said.

We all listened. It was like a pack of little dogs yapping. Presently we heard Dinky and Jody, screaming like Indians. Down the hill came a limping, lurching figure, strangely humped. He carried something in his arms, clasped to his chest.

Nursie sprang up. "My God!" he shouted. "Has he got your baby?"

The figure tripped and fell.

"He'll squash the baby," Nurse howled.

Jody and Dinky raced into view, pistol arms extended. They sprang on the prostrate man. The smell of ammonia filled the air.

Dad got up. He lifted up Dinky, then Jody. "All right," he said, "get up."

The figure humped itself tiredly and sat up. He turned a dirty, young face to us. His eyes were streaming from the ammonia and he looked tired to death. With a weary gesture he picked Fred up and threw him at Dinky.

"You horrible child," he said.

"Ye gods," said Nursie, "a doll! What is this?"

"All right," Dad said again, "get up now. I've had about enough of this. Who are you anyway?"

"Me?" the fellow said.

"Yes, you. What's your name?"

"Fred."

12

I F MOM was shocked when she opened the door and saw us standing there, she gave no sign of it. She just grabbed Jody and Dinky and hugged them, and then stood there looking blankly at big Nursie, now pretty well smeared with blood and no longer trying to be ladylike, at poor Fred, or whoever he was, who looked like a blond zombie and smelled quite a bit of ammonia, and at Dad, with his bloody face and black eye.

"Do come in," she said formally, and then, to Susan, "Run up and get the bath ready for these two."

"Come in, come in," Dad said heartily. "Come in by the fire. This is Officer Schulberg, who nursed us through the evening, and this is, er, Fred. My wife, Mrs. Evans." He waved his hands at each in turn.

"Fred looks awfully cold and miserable," Mom

said. "Take that chair by the fire, Fred. We'll have some dinner in a minute. Perhaps a drink — he really does look quite ill," she said to Dad. She kept on compulsively holding Dinky and Jody.

"Can I take my jacket off?" Jody said.

"Can I have something to eat?" Dinky said.

"May I," Mom said automatically. "Susan will give you a hot bath and then you can have dinner in your pajamas."

"You'll stay to dinner?" Mom asked, looking at Nursie and Fred.

"Thank you, no," Mr. Schulberg said. "I'm still on duty, working, that is. I better call in and have him picked up." He nodded toward Fred. "You'll want to prefer charges, I suppose. Has he done anything except steal the doll?"

"If it's all the same to you," Dad said, "I'd like to talk to him myself first. Fact is, we don't know what he's up to. Why don't I keep him here awhile and see if he'll talk?"

"Do you think he's a little — ?" Officer Schulberg twiddled his fingers near his forehead.

Dad raised his eyebrows and shrugged. "Well —" he said, "anyway I want to talk to him and I think my kids know something. We'll have some dinner and get to the bottom of this and I'll call you or you can give me a buzz later."

"Well, I guess that's all right," Mr. Schulberg said reluctantly. "A little irregular. I guess you can handle him. He looks harmless enough now." Fred did, indeed, look as limp as an angleworm.

"One thing," Officer Schulberg went on. "He hasn't any weapons. It was the kids had the weapons. That's irregular too. Probably illegal. If I were you I'd throw away those squirt guns and the ammonia too."

Dad and Mr. Schulberg walked to the door together, where they paid each other several compliments, appeared about to break into war stories but desisted, shook hands several times, and finally said goodbye.

"Well, that was quite an experience," Dad said, coming back. "Can't imagine what the kids thought of it. You'd better come and eat, Fred, and we'll talk later." You could see that Dad was so pleased with having been in a fight, at his age, and having gotten Jody and Dinky back too, that he felt kindly toward the whole world. Kate and Dave felt the same. In fact, as Dave said, he could feel his shoe-button eyes twinkling and his candy heart beating with happiness.

We all trooped in and sat around the dining-room table. Dad poured some strong drink from the brown bottle on the sideboard for Fred, and after that Fred got some color in his face and perked up and ate a little. We couldn't have been gone so very long because the lamb was hardly dried out at all. Susan had nervously beat the potatoes several times and they were gloriously fluffy. There is nothing like potatoes and gravy for starvation. Dave and Kate were passing back their plates for seconds before Dad was through carving. Dinky and Jody arrived, pink and clean in their nightclothes, and were clamoring for their dinners.

"Can't I have three bites?" Dad was saying. It was all just like home, and we all ate as much as Mr. Pickwick.

"I don't think I can wait any longer for this story," Mom said at last. "We can have coffee in the living room, and as it's very late, you older kids had better start your homework now."

We started to protest, but then found that Dad and Mom were both watching Fred. We watched him too. He was looking around the room, at the carved molding, the plate rail, the window seat, the paneling. His eyes roved and then stopped, as in recognition, and he was smiling a little. Then he leaned over and looked under the table. Dinky looked under the table too.

"Looking for something?" Dad said.

"The bell," Fred said, "to call the maid, you know. It's there, all right. The Stanhopes had a dog," he went on, smiling rather foolishly, "who dug up the bell and shorted the wires and the bell kept ringing in the kitchen."

"But you can't be *that* Fred," Mom said. "You're too young."

"No, that was Grandpa," Fred said. "When I was a boy in Alaska he used to come stay with us. I had a broken leg once, and he sat by my bed and told me stories about this house and the Stanhope kids. I didn't really believe him. We had a four-room house in the bush and it was hard to imagine a place as big as this. I was an only child and we lived pretty isolated. It was nice to hear about a big family."

"Come on in the living room," Mom said, "and tell us about it." We all trailed along after them and she forgot to send us out.

"What I want to know," Dad said, "is why on earth you've been taking Dinky's gingerbread man."

"He had the key," Fred said. "The gingerbread man, I mean. Sewed up inside him."

"What key is that?"

"The key to Grandfather's black box."

"Start at the beginning," Mom said.

"Well, you see," Fred said, "when the Stanhopes went bust and went back East, Grandpa came back up to Alaska. He and Grandma had had a falling-out years before and he left her and my dad, who was little then, and came down here. But when he went back to Alaska they made it up and he stayed there. He had a box with a key that he kept things in, and he left that here. He expected to be traveling and didn't want to bother with it. Mr. Stanhope said he'd put it in the safe for him, and some aunt or someone would be living here. They weren't going to sell the

144

house. In fact, Grandpa always thought they'd come back. There wasn't anything in the box of any value. Mr. Stanhope gave him some stock, but he said it wasn't worth anything, so Gramps put that in the box too."

"Aha!" Dad said.

"Then sometime later he got a letter from the youngest Stanhope boy, who was only ten or so and a great kidder, I guess, saying that he had Grandpa's key to the black box but not to worry because he had hidden it in Fred with the other keys. I guess this is a pretty silly-sounding story."

"Go on," Mom said.

"So Grandpa looked and he didn't have the key. Gramps was a pretty careless guy and he figured the box didn't matter much anyway. Then later on when he started to get the dividend checks, he got curious and wrote to Mr. Stanhope. Mr. Stanhope wrote back that the box was still in the safe in the Seattle house and said Grandpa could have it sent if he wanted. But living where he did and Grandpa being sort of suspicious of everyone, including the post office, he never sent for it. When he died a couple of years ago, he still hadn't got it. Mom and Dad were dead by that time too, and I was in the service.

"Well, I guess it was pretty silly. I mean maybe I was a little crazy. Been shot at too much or something. When I got out of the service I had no folks and no place to go, and I got to thinking of Gramp's stories. Besides, the black box was mine now, and I got it into my head I had to find it. I suppose there's some way of getting new stock certificates for lost ones. There must be some record. There were some other little things in the box too, just family things, but I wanted them. I thought I'd come here and see the house anyway. I thought from what Grandpa said that there would probably be Stanhopes living here. But there wasn't anyone. The house was empty. I went to see the realtor. He thought I was crazy, but I could see he was curious about the safe. Probably thought there'd be other things in it. He came here with me and we looked."

"Where is it?" Dave asked. "I've never seen any safe."

"That's just it," Fred said. "There isn't one. We looked and looked. It must have been the kind you could move. It must have been taken away."

"That's what we thought about the Room of the Eyes," Susan said, "but that was here."

"So what did you do?" Dave asked.

"I just decided I'd look for myself," Fred said. "I didn't have anyplace to go so I moved in here. I knew all about it. Grandpa had described everything. I knew how to get up on the roof and down into that room and I knew the way in through the ballroom. I just lived here and looked. When you folks moved in I stayed on. I didn't do any harm. I never found

146

the safe, but I found the gingerbread man. He was in that cupboard in the basement."

"Why didn't you take the key then?" Kate said.

"I didn't know which one it was," Fred said. "He's full of keys, you know."

"Keys!" Dinky said. "Those are his bones."

"I thought I'd keep him until I found the box," Fred said. "I was taking him up to my room that night when you kids came after me, and I dropped him."

"When was this?" Dad said.

"A long time ago," Susan said, "when we first moved in."

"I tried to get the little girl to give him up but she wouldn't. Then when you kids found the book and started on the treasure-hunting clues, I wanted to get him before you kids started ripping him up and losing my key. You know the book says, *From Fred, To Fred,* and there were those clues about *Ask Fred to bring the key.* I read the book, you know, but I didn't know about the Room of the Eyes."

"But we thought it was the other Fred," Susan said.

"Nobody is going to rip Fred up," Dinky said.

"How did you know about the clues?" Kate asked.

"I listened," Fred said. "That's how I knew you were going to the Market too. I didn't mean to frighten the little girl, but she's a holy terror, she is."

"How is it I don't know anything about these clues?" Dad said. "Or the room on the roof? Do you know?" he asked Mom. She shook her head.

"You tell me," he said to Susan, so Susan went up to her room and got all the clues and told the whole story.

"I can hardly believe it," Mom said. "All those years ago. A children's game, imagine. Doesn't it all seem real? I can just see those children, hiding things and playing games, perhaps right in this very room."

"Stealing Fred's key!" Dave said.

"What was the last clue again, Susan?" Dad asked. And Susan read:

> *Hot grow I, very hot,*
> *Yet I can't burn.*
> *Safe in the brick am I,*
> *Safe in the stone.*
> *Covered with ——— paper,*
> *Flowers and phlox,*
> *There lie I, there lie I,*
> *Safe in a box.*
> *Under the icing,*
> *Pink icing has Fred,*
> *There is the key to me*
> *Safe in his head.*

But Mom had her eye on Dinky and Jody, who were asleep, and on Fred, who was sagging like an empty coat.

"I think," she said, "that it's bedtime. Dave, you can sleep in Kate's other bed for tonight and Fred can have your room. You older kids get started on your homework, while I take Fred and the children up."

She didn't suggest that Fred go up to his room under the roof and he didn't mention it either. He followed her as docilely as Jody and Dinky and left the rest of us to silence and the books.

But later on, as Kate crept into bed, in the midst of thinking what an interesting day it had been and trying to remember that last clue, she suddenly thought, But why should they try to keep us out of the park? It's our park as much as theirs! We're only trying to get along and we don't want to hurt anyone. Why is everyone after us? Why do people hit our brothers and frighten our little sister and, as far as that goes, why should Linda call me "white girl" and the teacher get mad at me and everyone tease me about things I can't help? Why can't people leave us alone?

"Doesn't it seem," she said to Dave, "that ever since we moved to the city someone's been after us? The house doesn't like us, they don't like us very well at school, that fellow is still after you and Jody, those men in the park tried to chase us out."

"Oh, pooh," Dave said, "those men in the park don't like anybody. We're getting along better in school all the time. And as for the house not liking us, well, that was just Fred and we know about him now."

"Yes," Kate said, "but I feel as though the Stanhopes were looking over our shoulders all the time." It was true that things were getting better at school. They've got to get better, she thought wildly. I've got to be liked, I must be liked, I can't stand it otherwise!

How happy Dave looks, she thought. Dave was asleep and smiling. He was running, dreaming, through a green meadow, where golden boys threw golden balls and flashing swords kept evil men at bay.

Kate was asleep. Dinky was asleep. Beside her Fred's eyes shone in the darkness. The other Fred, Jody, May and Susan were asleep. We didn't hear Mom and Dad tapping at the fireplace walls, tapping at the foundations, poking around the furnace, looking for hollow noises. They gave up at last, and all was dark and quiet in the house on Capitol Hill.

13

THE DAYS went by, and Fred stayed with us. We had, as Dave said, a resident ghost. He came in very handy anyway, doing some painting and fixing leaky taps and tiling one of the bathrooms. He and Dinky became fast friends, and she followed him around all day. Mom got a cot and fixed up one of the third-floor rooms for him. We thought he might go to the University later on. Mom said the war had been very hard on him and she personally thought fighting should be left to older men like Dad and Officer Schulberg, who appeared to enjoy it.

Mom was pretty crabby about this time because she was dieting. She was very critical of Susan and Dave, who were growing rather fat, and also of Kate and Fred, who she felt were too thin. What with feeding up part of us and withholding food from the rest, she created a lot of tension. Dad too was preoccupied. Of course men, as Mom is always telling us, lead difficult lives, having to work every day and spend a lot of time in conferences and do paper work at night. Also if anything goes wrong, apparently someone has to take the blame. We think there are days when everyone says, "Darn it, Evans, you designed that airplane and the wings fell off!" This was evidently one of the bad times. What with one thing and another we children were left to cope with our own lives at this time without interference from above.

Susan spent hours working on the Stanhope code. She often laughed aloud as she translated, and remarked once that many of the people now living in tranquil and respectable old age up and down the street would be jolted by this account of their early years.

"I'll probably have to wait till they're dead to publish it," she said. Susan was doing almost no homework, only now and then dashing off enough to keep the school from calling Mom. She and Fred spent a lot of time looking for concealed safes.

May was almost living at the Wongs'. She took to eating out of a lot of little dishes and was always wanting to play Mah-Jong. When not being Chinese she lay on her bed, reading. Dave spent all his spare time with his new friends. He gave up all intellectual activities, never read anything, and was only interested in athletics. He was developing, Susan and Kate agreed, a wholesome, stupid look, like a golden Labrador.

Katie was learning (but how painfully!) how to get along, and she had, wonder of wonders, two good friends. One was the girl she had noticed the first day of school, the one who looked so rich. Her name was Sheila Canfield and she belonged to one of those families with a great deal of shy and unobtrusive wealth. That is, they never mentioned it, but it stuck out all over them. The other friend was Linda. Linda was as mean as ever, but Kate couldn't help liking her and Linda, strangely enough, liked Kate. One afternoon Kate went over to Linda's house after school to play.

"Where do you live?" she asked as they started out.

"I live in Coon Hollow, baby," Linda said. "I live in a slum."

"Coon Hollow isn't a slum," Kate said. She was sorry right after she'd said it. Nobody said "Coon Hollow" any more than they said "nigger toes" for Brazil nuts or "Eeny meeny miny mo, catch a nigger by the toe." They said "catch a little boy" now. Coon Hollow was called that because in the early days of Seattle it was full of raccoons, but now, since almost every house had a Negro family in it, it wasn't considered polite to say "Coon Hollow." Probably it was all right for Negroes to say it, just the way Poles could call themselves "dumb Polacks" and Jews could tell those jokes about themselves.

They went down the other side of Capitol Hill, away from town, passing streets of great big houses and then blocks of apartments and finally, after a good long walk downhill, coming to Coon Hollow. It was exactly like a small town. The hills rising around cut it off from the rest of the city and the trees obliterated the surrounding houses. Every yard had fruit trees and flowers and most of them had picket fences. The houses were small and old and each one was different. Some had bay windows, one had a little tower, and there were strangely sloping roofs and little sheds. Seen from a distance, the narrow streets with the bright-colored houses were home-like and even picturesque. Close to, many of the houses were seen to be tumbling down, with broken windows and overgrown yards. Others were spruce and neat, with fresh paint and shiny windows.

They passed a secondhand store with goods displayed on the sidewalk. There was an old black wood-burning cookstove and a lot of kitchen chairs.

"Who would buy that stove?" Kate asked. "No one uses them any more, do they?"

"We have one," Linda said.

"I've always wanted one," Kate said honestly, but her heart sank a little. She'd said the wrong thing again. Linda was always kidding her or outsmarting her, and now Linda would think she was ignorant or a snob or both.

Linda's house turned out to be one of the

spruced-up ones. There was a wood stove in the kitchen, but it was polished like pewter and the whole house was very small and bright and homelike. It was in a state of sparkling cleanliness never achieved by the Evanses. In the street outside the house there was broken glass and, right in the middle, a high-heeled shoe.

"There was a fight here last night," Linda said as they skirted the glass and the shoe, "but it didn't have anything to do with us."

"We had a fight the other night," Kate said, and she told Linda about taking the swords and going up in the park.

"Weren't you afraid of the police?" Linda asked.

"Of course not," Kate said. "Why would we be?"

"If my family took swords or knives and went in the park, they'd arrest us," Linda said.

"But the police are supposed to help you look for lost children," Kate said.

"Sure, baby," Linda said. "You're kind of dumb, aren't you, Kate? You act like the police are on your side."

"Well, they are!" Kate said.

"Don't kid yourself," Linda said.

"Is your mom home?" Kate asked.

"No, she's still at work. She works at the hospital to buy my clothes," Linda said.

"Well, you have awfully pretty clothes," Kate said. She had often admired Linda's clothes, which were not only new and pretty, but seemed cleverly planned to suit her. She remembered that our mom had often talked of getting a job to buy things for the house.

"Come on," Linda said, "let's go out and find someone to play with." They went up and down the street and collected Linda's friends. Someone had a ball and they played squares. They climbed some trees and played tag and hide-and-seek. They were the kind of girls Kate liked. That is, they were all fast on their feet and gay and happy. They called her "white girl" of course, and she could see they were trying to wear her out, but she was used to Linda now and it didn't bother her very much.

But all the time, even when she was running, she kept thinking, how funny to be the only white person on the street. It gave her a strange feeling, not frightened, but lost. The street was full of children, all black, with grownups coming and going, all black. How I must stick out, she thought. What if I came here every day, and went to a Negro school; what if all the stores and movies and museums were run by Negroes. Wouldn't it feel odd? And yet Linda goes bravely every day into all-white neighborhoods. The school is integrated, of course, but what about the rest of the town?

And later on, that evening, in the middle of her homework, she thought she would like to ask Linda to stay overnight sometime. But then what if Linda asked her back? Would she want to stay at Linda's house, all alone, with no other white person within blocks? But what a terrible person I must be, to feel this way! What difference can skin make? Why are different people different colors anyway? There's enough trouble in the world without that. Surely God could see that He made a mistake, making people different colors, and do something about it.

Of course Dad would say that God didn't make people different colors, but that they evolved or mutated or something that way. Nobody's fault, then, not God's or people's, and nobody to blame, which makes it worse.

When Kate first visited at Sheila's house she felt stranger than she had at Linda's, but it was a strangeness that would be easy to get used to. Sheila lived in a beautiful modern house. The side away from the street was all glass and the mountains seemed to come right in the room. The furniture was partly modern, very low and comfortable, and partly antique Chinese. There was a swimming pool and almost a block of garden with a high fence around it. Right in the middle of the city!

"How come you don't go to a private school?" Kate said.

"Because Mom and Dad want me to learn to know all kinds of people and get along with everybody," Sheila said.

"Do you get along with everybody?" Kate asked curiously.

"I try," Sheila said, "but there are some people you can't get along with, aren't there? And there are lots of people who don't like me, no matter what I do."

"I'll tell you who I don't like," Kate said. They sat on the lovely squashy modern sofa and told each other who they didn't like. When they got through they both felt a lot better. I knew I'd been trying too hard, Kate thought, and from now on I'm not going to bother. People can like me or not as they please.

"Is it all right to climb those trees?" she said, looking out the windows.

"Yes," Sheila said, "let's go do it."

So Kate had two good friends and life was making some sense again. If only the Stanhopes would stop haunting us, she thought, everything would be all right.

But when she got home from Sheila's that night Dave's bicycle had been stolen, and while he was out looking for it that big dark boy caught him and he had another black eye.

14

WE COULDN'T tell Dad about the bicycle. He'd have flown right up in the air and said it was all Dave's fault. We knew that, he'd forgotten to lock it, but what good would it do to have Dad pointing it out? We told Fred instead. Fred was grown-up or at least old enough to have gone to war, but he had a rational, childish point of view. His idea was that we should simply go out and look for the bicycle.

"Some kids," he said, "just pick up a bike and ride it a few blocks and then drop it. Other kids just plain steal a bike and take it home. If either of these things happened, we might find it if we keep looking. Of course if someone stole it and sold it, then it may be in another part of town. But it won't hurt to look."

"What if we find it?" Kate asked.

"We steal it back," Fred said.

A very practical guy, Fred was. We loved him. Growing up in Alaska, he'd become a pioneer type, used to taking justice into his own hands.

We didn't find it the first day, but we kept looking. The next day Fred and Susan went to the library and on the way home they went around some blocks, looking for Dave's bike. They were walking along one of those streets that is partly apartment houses and partly regular houses. The regular houses were in bad shape, with a rugged, dazed look, like aristocrats waiting to go to the guillotine. Fred and Susan were walking slowly, sometimes going a little way up walks or driveways to look at parked bicycles, when they saw a terrible thing.

There was a big, square, turn-of-the-century house, almost like our house, and it was being torn down. The whole front of the house was gone, and you could see right inside, like the back of a doll house. There was a great big fireplace in the living room and it had a fire in it. The workmen were all standing around the fire eating their lunch. They looked very cozy as they poured coffee from their thermos jugs and took bites of sandwiches. Now and then one of them would pick up a piece of the house that was lying around and throw it on the fire.

"How terrible!" Susan gasped. "Look, they're making the house burn itself."

"I'll tell you what, Susan," Fred said. "Pretty soon

they'll get rid of all these big old houses and after that no one will remember what it was like to live in a proper house. Everyone will live in little boxes no bigger than log cabins."

"Not our house," Susan said stoutly.

"Hope not," Fred said. They stood there, looking in horror at the littered floor, the untouched woodwork, the scrolled wallpaper that hung down in streamers, the great cheerful fireplace.

"Look, Fred," Susan said. "Look up at the side of the chimney, above the mantelpiece."

"What is it?" Fred said. "Is it a door?" They moved closer. There was a little door. The wallpaper half covered it.

"It's a safe built into the chimney," Fred said, "so things would be safe even if the house burned down."

"Hot grow I, very hot, Yet I can't burn," Susan quoted. *"Safe in the brick am I, Safe in the stone."*

"Covered with WALL*paper,"* Fred said. "They put a blank because they knew wallpaper would give it away. It must be just like that one."

"Flowers and phlox," Susan said. "We haven't any flowered wallpaper. Come on, Fred, let's run home."

They ran all the way home and went, panting and hopeful, into the living room. The living-room walls were plastered and not even cracked. There was no place for a safe. So were the library walls.

"The bedrooms have painted walls too," Susan said, but they looked anyway.

"It's wallpaper painted over," Fred said. He was right. You could see the places where the paper lapped over. In Mom and Dad's room, on the side of the chimney above the mantel, you could feel the outline of a square. Fred traced it out with his finger. They couldn't see it, but you could feel a change in the surface. Fred didn't waste any time saying "What would your Mother say?" He just took out his jack-knife and cut the paper around. Then he pulled the paint and wallpaper loose and there was a metal door, not very big, with a keyhole in it.

Susan stood there, silent, and watched him. But when the keyhole appeared she positively jumped up and down.

"Fred has the key to me," she said. *"Safe in his head."*

"You better go get it," Fred said. "I'm not going to tangle with Dinky again."

"But she likes you now, Fred," Susan said.

"She may like me, but she won't let me touch Fred," Fred said, so Susan went in search of Dinky.

"Listen, Dinky," she said. "You know there are some keys sewed up inside Fred." Dinky rolled her eyes and held Fred tightly.

"Don't start crying," Susan said hastily. "All we want is the key to this little door we found. If you let us have the key we'll sew Fred up again and you'll never know he's been cut open."

"But it will hurt him terribly," Dinky said.

"He won't even feel it, I promise," Susan said.

"Let me see the door," Dinky said. Susan took her in and showed her the little door in the chimney.

"Hm-m," Dinky said, "now let's see the thread you'll sew him up with." Susan went away and found pink thread and brown thread.

"Please, Dinky," she said, "can't you see how anxious Fred and I are? Hurry up, for heaven's sake!"

"All right," Dinky said at last. "Go ahead, but I want to hold his hand."

"It's just under the velvet," Susan said. "That's what the clue says. *Under the icing, Pink icing has Fred, There is the key to me, Safe in his head.* See, you can feel the key in this stripe of velvet." Her scissors ripped up the piece of velvet and there was a little key.

"Here you go, Fred," she said.

"No, stop, get Fred sewed up first!" Dinky said.

"Oh, don't be silly, Dinky," Susan said. "We're in a hurry. Don't you want to know what's in the safe?"

But tears were starting in the daisy eyes.

"Never mind," Fred said. "Sew him up, Susan. We can wait that long." Susan was a fast sewer, and her quick needle stitched the pink band back on in a minute.

Fred took the key and unlocked the door. Inside was a good-sized cupboard, lined with metal, with a lead-colored shelf.

"What's in it?" Susan asked, craning to see over Fred's shoulder. "I can't see anything."

"There isn't anything," Fred said. "No box anyhow. We've been tricked again."

"There must be a clue," Susan said. "Isn't there even a piece of paper? Feel up on the top shelf."

Fred felt around. "Yes, there is," he said. He pulled out an envelope and a note.

"Here's your clue," he said, handing the note to Susan. He still held the envelope in his hand. "And this envelope says, *To Fred.*"

"Open it quick," Susan said, "it ought to explain."

"*Dear Fred,*" read Fred, "*this is just a quick note to tell you that we have moved your box. It did seem a shame, when we planned such a nice place for our own things, not to have yours with them. We talked about it, Paul and I, and finally we got the key to this safe off Dad's key ring. Then we got your box and put it with our toys and hid the key to it in Fred. To find it you can follow the treasure-hunt clues that begin in the book in the secret room. But perhaps that won't be necessary. Maybe we will come back and you will come back and we will all live merrily together again. Anyway, the best of luck to the best treasure-hunter of them all, our dear friend Fred, from your true friend George.*"

"Isn't that something?" Fred said. "If I had that kid here, I'd wring his neck!"

"Oh, Fred, you wouldn't attack an old man, would you?" Susan said.

"Old man? Oh, I see what you mean. I was thinking he was still a boy," Fred said. "He'd only be middle-aged."

"Well, even so you wouldn't attack him," Susan said. "I think it's kind of sweet. Sort of like Jody. He was so sure Fred would want his box to be with their things and he was sure Fred would want to play this last game. He must have lived in a very secure world."

"It may be sweet," Fred said, "but I'll never care much for him. Go on, read the clue. We may beat the little rat yet."

Susan read from the note she'd been holding:

We're walled up and closed up, we're still, dusty, dumb.
We'll sit here in the darkness and wait for you to come.
Tap on the walls, follow the floors,
It's hollow as a drum.
Hammer and chisel, high and low,
Down come the walls of Jericho!

"*Walled up,*" repeated Fred. "That sounds as though they made a false wall. But they didn't. There isn't a room in this house with a false wall."

"There must be," Susan said. "We haven't looked

well enough. Maybe in the basement. After all," she said reasonably, "everything else they've said has come true."

"I've been over this house foot by foot," Fred said. "What kind of a wall would those kids put up? This great kidder George, now, can you see him putting up a wall that would fool us? It wasn't as if Gramps had been there to help them."

"Maybe there was a carpenter here then," Susan said. "Someone crating up things or something. Lizzy might know. He might have helped them."

"Maybe," Fred said, "the only thing to do is just what the clue said. Knock on the walls, hunt around. What's that?"

"Fred, Susan," Kate was calling, "where are you?" She and Dave came thundering up the stairs.

"Guess what!" Dave said. "We've found it!"

"We found the bike," Kate said. "What about it, Fred? Can we steal it back?"

"We can and we will," Fred said firmly. "First, case the joint. Would it be better to wait till dark? Or would a thief be careful enough to put his bike away at night?"

"Let's go now," Dave said, "and see if the coast is clear."

They went, the four of them.

"If no one's around, I'll steal it," Fred said. "They can't hurt me. We can prove it's ours, I suppose? The parents might not know it was stolen."

"I've got the fender that got bent. I took it off a month ago," Dave said.

"Good," Fred said.

It was a simple thing, after all. Stealing is as easy as shelling peas, only when you get through shelling peas you don't feel guilty. Fred got that bicycle off someone's side porch without making a sound, and when Dave put it away in the back hall at home we all felt relieved of an immense burden.

"The only thing is," Dave said to Kate when they were doing their homework that evening, "I feel funny, as though I'd stolen his bicycle instead of him stealing mine. I know it's mine and I have a right to it, but I feel guilty."

For Susan and Fred the bicycle had been an unimportant interlude. They were tapping on walls and looking at floorboards.

"Sounds like the shoemaker and the elves around here," Dad said.

"Fred cut a hole in your room," Dinky said.

"What!" Dad said.

"He cut a hole in your room and Susan cut a hole in Fred, but she sewed that up. The one in your room is still there, with a dear little gray shelf in it."

"What!" Dad said. "Fred! Susan! Stop acting like water dowsers and come down here. Dave! Kate!"

"He's found out about the bike!" Dave said.

But when everyone was assembled (Mom and Jody came too) he only wanted to know what Dinky meant, so Susan told him about the safe and read the clue again:

We're walled up and closed up, we're still, dusty,
    dumb.
We'll sit here in the darkness and wait for you to
    come.
Tap on the walls, follow the floors,
It's hollow as a drum.
Hammer and chisel, high and low,
Down come the walls of Jericho!

So we all started tapping around, but for a long time nothing came of it.

»»»»» **15** «««««

THERE FOLLOWED a long quiet time, maybe two weeks.

Nothing was stolen, there were no more black eyes, we had no prowlers. Nobody seemed to be after us at all. We didn't find any walled-up rooms either, though we tapped industriously and Susan's knuckles got so sore she took to tapping with a cane.

"If you wore a long cape and black glasses, you'd look just like Blind Pew," Dave said.

We wended our way peacefully through these two weeks and reached the second Saturday. It was a beautiful morning, blue and sunny. We were all waiting around for Mom to assign jobs or let us out of them. Dinky and Jody were still asleep, Fred was up in his bedroom, Kate and May were out in the yard, Dad and Dave were out in the car, just going to the hardware store, Susan was in the living room, and Mom was in the kitchen.

There was no wind, the leaves hung still. The street was empty, the sky was empty, there was no warning.

Then there was a grumbling, a rumbling, growing louder, vaster, more ominous, a mighty rumbling. It came from all over. It was loudest over our heads. With it went many rattles, higher-pitched, faster than the rumbling. The horrid unbelievable sound went on and on, while the floor heaved like the sea.

Mom thought, The house is coming down, and then she thought, No, the furnace is blowing up. She started toward the basement door and then she thought, Why should I go down there? I can't stop it. She came back toward the front of the house. Kate and May came in the front door.

"The ground is going up and down, so we came in," they said.

"Come here, under the stairs," Mom said. "I guess it's an earthquake."

The three of them stood together under the stairs.

"There's nothing to be afraid of," Mom said, but the rumbling went on.

Susan sat still in the living room. She watched the pictures sliding back and forth on the walls and the vases on the mantelpiece rocking. She heard the windows rattling in their frames. The lamps rocked

on the tables and the chandeliers swung like censers.

Jody's door opened. "What's going on?" he said.

"It's only an earthquake," Susan said.

"Oh, is that all," Jody said, and went back to bed.

Susan looked outside. The sun shone benignly. An innocent golden haze enveloped the air.

Then it was all over. The rumbling stopped. The pictures stopped moving, the vases and windows were silent. The whole house rocked to a standstill and everything was solid and safe again. Dad and Dave came in.

"The road was snapping like a whip," Dad said. "Any damage? I'd better look at the chimneys."

"Mrs. Evans," Fred was calling, "something came to pieces up here. One of the chimneys must be down."

Dinky appeared on the stairs in her bathrobe.

"What are you doing?" she said severely. "Fred nearly fell out of bed."

Fred came into the hall. He was pale and shaky and looked frightened.

"Something was falling all around me," he said. "It was like being shelled."

"I will never get used to earthquakes," Mom said. "At least in the Middle West when we have a tornado it gets dark. It's unnatural for the sun to shine."

"Boy, was I scared," Kate said. "I thought the ground was going to break open and I'd fall in the hole."

"I thought the furnace was blowing up," Mom said.

We all talked at once, telling what we had thought.

"Let's look at those chimneys, Fred," Dad said, and we all followed him like the tail of a kite. We bunched in the third-floor hall while they went out on the roof.

"Only a couple of bricks lying around," Dad said. "You're shell-shocked, boy. We better go around and look at the others, though this is the one closest to your room."

"Come on," Dinky called. "There's a horse in here."

"Where is she?" Mom said.

"In the front bedroom, I think," Susan said.

"Come in here!" Dinky called. "It was the horse that made all the noise. He's knocked down a wall, trying to get out."

We all went in the front bedroom, the one Lizzy O'Leary said was the cook's room.

"Poor horse," Dinky was saying. "How mean to shut him up like that."

A part of the wall was half down. A horse's head, with a peculiar rakish expression, his forelock askew, looked over it. In the back of the exposed space, on high shelves, were many dolls, all dressed up and sitting like ladies in church, staring at us.

"My God," Dad said, "what is it? A family burying ground?"

But Fred and Susan were pulling the wall down. Two immense bookcases that were leaning against it fell forward into the room, flat on the floor on top of the flattened wall. The floor was littered with books. Their falling was what had frightened Fred, not bricks at all. The bookcases must have been tight against the wall and that was the reason, Fred said afterward, that the wall hadn't sounded hollow. When the earthquake started they rocked back and forth and battered the wall down. The little room (it was a walled-off alcove, really) was crammed tight, like a packing case. It was a treasure trove, like a Christmas catalog materialized.

The rocking horse was the kind that looks like a real horse. It was dapple-gray, with a long gray mane and tail. There was a puppet theater, with Punch and Judy reclining in a relaxed way on the stage. There was an electric train with enormous cars, a steam engine with a shiny tank and red pulleys, a castle with knights and horses, not plastic, but painted lead. There was a fortress too, with English lead soldiers and cannon, and a toy clipper ship. We saw an enormous doll house with the furniture in it and the little doll people all sitting around the table. There was a little Boston rocker, Dinky's size, a table and chairs, and a cupboard full of doll dishes. There were boxes of blocks, and little brassbound trunks full of doll clothes. Right in the middle, sitting on a wicker child's chair, was one of those long-legged floppy dolls that ladies in the twenties used to put on their beds. Her hair was stiffly waved, her face impossibly painted, and on her blue satin lap, on her boneless knees, was a black box with a red ribbon on it.

"There it is, Fred," Susan said.

There was a nursery clock too, with a face painted on it and blue nursery-rhyme pictures around the edge. The key to wind it with was, we supposed, in Fred. Dad pulled the rocking horse into the room and Dinky climbed on it. Dave handed her a baby doll and a teddy bear, and Fred pulled Fred from under her arm. She rocked on blissfully, and by the time she missed Fred, Susan and Fred had slit the velvet bands with Fred's razor blade and Fred had given up his keys. "Come, Fred, *give Fred what is his.*"

Mom was picking up the books and reading the titles.

"Look," she said, "bound volumes of *St. Nicholas.* And, see here, *The Motor Girls in Japan,* I read that when I was a little girl. *Dumps, a Plain Girl,* by Mrs. Meade. These A. A. Milne's are all first editions."

Dad held one of the lead soldiers in his hand. "I've always wanted a set of these," he said. "Is Jody here?" Jody was there. He had found a child's easel and was pulling at it, but he kept dropping it to look at the steam engine and the Erector Set.

It was a great day, the earthquake day, almost sheer

bliss. It was only later on that we discovered one of the lead pipes had broken. The water leaked down into the dining room and subsequently part of the dining-room ceiling came down.

This is what is meant by "You can't make an omelet without breaking eggs."

What would have happened if we'd never had the earthquake? Would we ever have found those toys? The Stanhopes had done a good job building that wall, and then the people before us had papered it over. We might never have found all those delightful toys and books, and Fred never have found his box. Maybe years from now, when someone wants another freeway, or when the urban renewal people decide that apartments are nicer than houses, our house will be torn down. Maybe they will set that awful ball banging against our house. Maybe then, if it hadn't been for the earthquake, the ball would beat against the rock-hard wall until it made a hole in the cook's old room, and the horse's head and all the round-eyed dolls and teddy bears would peer out at the wreckers as they did at us.

Epilogue

So THAT'S what happened when we moved to the city. Just a rainbow and an earthquake. That isn't much, is it? It could happen to anyone. It just changed our whole lives, that's all, and we're different people, although it would be hard to say just how. A big, shapeless lump of experience, that's what we've got, and what it consists of we don't quite know.

Put it this way: we're just not so dumb anymore. We know that rich is richer than we thought and poor is poorer. For instance, when we were visiting our old friends a while ago and Dave told about his bicycle being stolen, one of the kids said, "Why would anyone steal a bicycle? Everyone has one."

We're not that dumb anymore.

We know that the world is strange and perilous, without logic. At least our house is our own, at last.

It gave us a present. We belong here. The Stanhopes don't hang over us anymore, although we know they'll never be entirely gone. Bits of the house belong to them, and to Lizzy O'Leary, and Fred, and that other Fred.

Our Fred is still with us. He's going to the University. He has his stock certificates and also, what he seems to value more, a portrait of his grandmother as a girl, some baby pictures of his father, and a diary his grandfather kept when he was prospecting in Alaska.

It's November now. The rains have begun. Thin veils of mist hang between our house and the one next door. The sky is soft and gray and fits down on us like a ceiling, shutting out the mountains and the Sound. No longer is it necessary to visit with the neighbors. Windows need not be washed; it is hardly necessary even to dust. Just throw another log on the fire and be happy. Strange, we pride ourselves on Seattle's beauty, we brag about the scenery, but we feel most normal when we can't see it, when the drifting veils of rain fall between us and our incredible views. Outside, the air is moist and scentless, the laurel, the ivy and the holly wax fat and green.

And what happened to the large dark boy who menaced our brothers? He came rushing up on our lawn one day and said, "We're moving to Tacoma and I'll never see you again, Dave Evans, and boy, am I glad!" Boy, are we glad too! This may sound like an anticlimax, but it was a relief anyway. He went rushing off, taking his furious guilt with him, and good riddance.

So here we are at home, we Evanses, lying on the living-room floor in front of the fire, with the doors locked and the whole rainy city outside. This is the end of the book, throw another log on the fire . . . Ugh! Homework!